Take
She's Mine

A Comedy in Two Acts

by Phoebe and Henry Ephron

A SAMUEL FRENCH ACTING EDITION

SAMUEL FRENCH

FOUNDED 1830

New York Hollywood London Toronto

SAMUELFRENCH.COM

TAKE HER, SHE'S MINE

Presented by Harold S. Prince at The Biltmore Theatre, New York City, December 21, 1961. Staged by George Abbott. Settings and lighting by William and Jean Eckart. Costumes by Florence Klotz.

THE CAST

PRINCIPAL	*Nicholas Saunders*
MOLLIE MICHAELSON	*Elizabeth Ashley*
FRANK MICHAELSON	*Art Carney*
ANNE MICHAELSON	*Phyllis Thaxter*
LIZ MICHAELSON	*June Harding*
AIRLINE CLERK	*Ron Welsh*
EMMETT	*Stephen Paley*
ADELE McDOUGALL	*Jean McClintock*
SARAH WALKER	*Louise Sorel*
DONN BOWDRY	*Tom Brannum*
1ST FRESHMAN	*Marty Huston*
2ND FRESHMAN	*Ron Welsh*
RICHARD GLUCK	*Walter Moulder*
ALFRED GREIFFINGER	*Paul Geary*
ALEX LOOMIS	*Richard Jordan*
MR. WHITMYER	*Heywood Hale Broun*
LINDA LEHMAN	*Susan Stein*
CLANCY	*Joe Ponazecki*
MR. HIBBETTS	*Ferdi Hoffman*

The action of the play takes place in Southern California and New England.

THE TIME
The present.

ACT ONE
A year ago.

ACT TWO
Now.

3

Take Her, She's Mine

ACT ONE

TIME: *A year ago.*

SETTING: *The Stage will be divided into several playing areas, all very flexible and indicated by as few light portable props as are needed to convey the setting to the audience. At the extreme Left, a telephone pole carries a tangle of telephone wires across the stage, quite high up, to connect with another telephone pole, Stage Right. Stage Right is Southern California, where the Michaelson family lives, and Stage Left is the east, where MOLLIE goes to college. From time to time, as indicated in the action, the Michaelson living room will appear at Right, and the dormitory room will appear at Left. Center Stage will be a general playing area which will vary in nature by the use of small backdrops, which will lower in, or appropriate props. Whenever the action shifts from one portion of the Stage to another, the lights will go out on the section of the stage not being used. This direction will not be repeated in the course of the play, but will be taken for granted. The back wall will be a sky drop.*

AT RISE: *A high school graduation is going on, Stage Center. A man who looks like a school PRINCIPAL is calling names and handing out imaginary diplomas to imaginary girls and boys, whose names he calls out. On a step slightly above him and to one side is MOLLIE MICHAELSON, in white cap and gown. As each name is called, MOLLIE moves one step to the side, closer to the PRINCIPAL, preparatory to coming down the step and receiving her diploma. MOLLIE is almost eighteen, intelligent, alert, enthusiastic, with the look of a young woman who has had everything proper—from tooth-straightening to dancing classes —done for her. The rest of the Michaelson family— FRANK, ANNE and LIZ—are seated to one side, watching the ceremony. FRANK and ANNE are an attractive couple in their early forties and very youngish looking. Their daughter LIZ is about fifteen, still gangly and awkward, but showing promise that she will one day be a beauty.*

PRINCIPAL. (*Reading from a list.*) Dorothy Lewkins. . . . (*The imaginary Dorothy Lewkins is handed an imaginary diploma, and the* PRINCIPAL *pantomimes a handshake.* MOLLIE *moves one step closer, as there is a spatter of APPLAUSE.* MOLLIE *looks at family—smiles.*) Judith Markowitz. . . . (*Same business.*) Frederick Arthur Meadows, Jr., Fidelis Award. (*Same business, with a little more enthusiastic APPLAUSE.* MOLLIE *is now next, up on the step.*) Mollie Michaelson. . . . (*Gets diploma. The* PRINCIPAL *pauses impressively, as* MOLLIE *comes down the step to him, smiling a delightfully wide smile.*) Ephebian, Sealbearer, Fidelis Award—and now receiving the Gold Cord for Scholarship. (*He drapes the imaginary gold cord around* MOLLIE'S *neck, shakes her hand, and she exits, as the audience, especially the* MICHAELSONS, *are heard applauding enthusiastically. As the LIGHTS dim out* FRANK *walks to the proscenium, Stage Left, and looks out at the audience.*)

FRANK. That's my daughter. When it's your own daughter, and she gets all those— (*Emotion makes him stop for a moment, to collect himself.*) I had some idea of how the president's mother and father felt the day he was inaugurated. That may be a somewhat exaggerated comparison. Still I don't think you have to be too modest. After all it was only eighteen years ago—seventeen and a half to be exact—we brought home from the hospital a five-pound bundle no bigger than a chicken you get at the supermarket—and there was that five-pound bundle up there with a smile on her face that would— (*Breaks off again.*) Anyway, it's quite clear that we've got a "Brain." And that imposes an obligation on you. Now, more than ever, the world is being shaped by ideas. And Mollie might just possibly be one of those people who— (*Stops, and comes down to earth.*) So we were very pleased when Mollie got into a good eastern college. As a matter of fact she had her choice of four. She elected to go to "Hawthorne College for Women." Hawthorne College has a student body of two thousand. It is located in Massachusetts, and it's bounded on the east by the Atlantic Ocean, on the west by Harvard, on the north by Dartmouth, and on the south by Yale. It's supposed to be a good location. Well, I won't bore you with what it costs to send a child to college these days. I'll only tell you it comes to a little more than twice what Annie and I lived on the first year we were married. But I'm not complaining. I can afford it. I got into plastics early. I've done very well. Mollie isn't the "Brain" by accident. There's *something* to be said for the genes. (*He beams at himself and the world.*) Anyway, we'll have an extra expense. We live in Southern California, so about four times a year we'll find ourselves at the Los Angeles International Airport. I don't know how about you, but I'll never get used to airplane travel. It's not so bad when you're going by yourself. You're too busy to be nervous. But when you're seeing somebody else off, and she's not quite eighteen years old, and it's the first time— We-ell— (FRANK *exits Stage Left.*)

(*Stage Center, an AMERICAN AIRLINE ARRIVAL AND DEPARTURE SIGN appears. Various flight numbers and times are indicated on it. In a moment,* MOLLIE, ANNE *and* LIZ *enter Stage Right and look up at the sign.* ANNE *and* LIZ *are dressed California style, rather casually.* MOLLIE *is wearing a traveling suit and hat. She carries a coat over her arm and a book and some magazines in her other arm.* ANNE

*carries still another coat and a small dressing case.
LIZ holds a box of cookies, and a large, shapeless bag,
stuffed to capacity. She sets the bag down. No one
but our principals will be seen in this scene, but there
is a hubbub of VOICES and the muted sound of
PLANES taking off and arriving.)*

ANNE. What's the number of your flight, Mollie?

MOLLIE. Thirty-six.

LIZ. Gate Seven—it's on time.

ANNE. I'm sure I should have something profound to
say to you—but I can't for the life of me think what.

MOLLIE. Don't worry, Mom. Daddy will have something profound to say to me.

LIZ. Well, this isn't very deep, but I'll miss you, Mollie.

MOLLIE. Me too, Liz.

(The TWO GIRLS *kiss.* ANNE *starts to sniffle.)*

ANNE. I'm going to cry.

MOLLIE. For heaven's sake, Mom, you cried all through
the packing. *(She waves to somebody evidently going
past.)* Hi, Lucy! You on Flight Thirty-six? *(The answer
is apparently in the affirmative.)* Good! See you on the
plane.

ANNE. *(Watching the non-existent Lucy's departure.)*
Who's Lucy?

MOLLIE. Lucy Shanks. She's going to Smith.

ANNE. She's wearing that suit you tried on at Mag-
nin's.

MOLLIE. Well, now will you admit I didn't make a
mistake?

*(*FRANK *comes* D. L. *into scene, looking as if he has been
running.)*

FRANK. Where the hell have you been? I've been looking all over the airport for you.

MOLLIE. *(Crosses to* FRANK.*)* Daddy, I'm traveling

American Airlines. We're right in front of the counter. Where else would we be?

FRANK. Oh. (*A small voice.*) I thought it was United.

ANNE. Calm down, dear. (*She joins* LIZ, *leaving* FRANK *and* MOLLIE *together.*)

FRANK. Checked in, Mollie?

MOLLIE. Yes, Daddy.

FRANK. Good seat?

MOLLIE. By the window.

FRANK. Any overweight?

MOLLIE. No.

(FRANK *looks at* MOLLIE, *love and affection shining in his eyes. He puts his hands on* MOLLIE'S *shoulders.* ANNE *and* LIZ *exchange looks of "he's off again," and stand back and listen.*)

FRANK. Now listen, Mollie, you're being given a great opportunity. It isn't every girl who gets it. Not that you haven't earned it. But, in its own way, Hawthorne is in a class with great schools like Harvard, Yale, Oxford. Now you've got the mind to take this opportunity and— (*He breaks off as* MOLLIE *spots somebody over his shoulder and waves gaily.*)

MOLLIE. Hi, Roger! You on Flight Thirty-six? (*Waits for an answer.*) Good! See you on the plane.

(ALL, *except* FRANK, *watch the departure of the nonexistent Roger.*)

ANNE. Who's that?

MOLLIE. (*Crosses to* ANNE.) Roger Ezor. He got into Dartmouth—to everybody's surprise, including his own.

FRANK. Mollie—

MOLLIE. (*Obediently; goes back to* FRANK.) Yes, Daddy. I have a very fine mind and a very fine opportunity.

FRANK. Well, what I mean is, make use of it. Make use of it to the fullest extent. So that in later years you won't feel that you wasted a great opportunity and we won't feel that all this money is going just for— (*He sees the enormous bag behind* MOLLIE *and stops short.*) That bag? I thought you were checked through.

MOLLIE. I'm taking that on the plane with me.

FRANK. (*He goes to bag, picks it up and feels its weight.*) Are you crazy? They won't let you get away with that.

MOLLIE. (*With great patience.*) Will you please stop worrying, Daddy? Anybody who weighs as little as I do shouldn't have to pay overweight. (*Whispers.*) Look at that man— (*Indicates:* ALL *look.*) two hundred and fifty pounds, if he weighs an ounce. Is he being charged for his overweight?

FRANK. But suppose they don't let you through with that?

MOLLIE. They won't even see it. After I'm through the gate all you have to do is hand it to me over the fence. (FRANK *drops the bag with a thud.*) It's common practice. (*Waves to someone.*) Hi, Joycie. Hello, Mr. and Mrs. Kincaid. (*Joycie and the Kincaids have evidently stopped.*) I'd like you to meet my parents—and my sister, Elizabeth. (FRANK, ANNE *and* LIZ *all murmur "how-do-you-do."*) Joycie is going to Hawthorne, too. (ANNE *and* FRANK *warm up genially in the presence of these equally fortunate parents.*)

ANNE. Well, how nice.

MOLLIE. (*Moves to Stage Left, confines her remarks to Joyce.*) Joycie, what do you think? Roger broke off with Alice! . . . Right after Brenda's party. . . . Well, it never would have lasted anyway, what with her going to Cal and him at Dartmouth. (*Laughs.*)

ANNE. I suppose we'll be seeing a lot of each other in the next four years.

FRANK. At the airport, anyway. (*Listens to something Mr. Kincaid is evidently saying.*) Yes, I guess we *can* be very proud of them.

MOLLIE. Say, you'd better hurry. Most of the good seats are gone already.

FRANK. Very nice to have met you, too. We'll look forward to seeing you again—er—just before Christmas. (*He is beaming as the Kincaids take off.*) Now what was I talking about?

LIZ. The challenge of the future.

(MOLLIE *comes back to* FRANK.)

FRANK. Oh, yes. (*Pulls himself together.*) Look, Mollie, you can go to college and just have a good time. Lots of people do it and there isn't anything really wrong with it. But these are the times—

MOLLIE. (*She suddenly remembers something, and smites herself on the brow. Crossing to* LIZ.) Liz! I forgot my black strapless bra. It's on my dresser.

LIZ. (*Cutting in.*) If you're the smartest one in this family, why do you always forget everything?

FRANK. (*Also cutting in.*) Mollie, I'm trying to tell you something that's vital.

MOLLIE. (*Without looking at him.*) Yes, Daddy. Now, Liz, there are three dresses that absolutely *need* that bra, so you won't forget to send it to me, will you?

FRANK. (*A subdued roar.*) I'll send you the black strapless bra if you'll just listen to me! (*This brings everybody round.* MOLLIE *marches back to stand and face her father.* FRANK *gets set to go into his speech again. They haven't seen him yet, but* EMMETT WHITMYER *has entered stage left, behind Frank.* EMMETT *is a gangling young man, attired in jeans and a tee shirt and scuffed sneakers. He is hopelessly in love with Mollie.*) Now, Mollie, you're taking a very important step in your life. These are the times—

EMMETT. (*Coming closer.*) That try men's souls.

(*They* ALL *turn and look at him.*)

FRANK. Oh. Hello, Paul.

MOLLIE. Not Paul, Daddy. Emmett.

FRANK. Emmett. Where are you going?

EMMETT. I'm not going anyplace, Mr. Michaelson. I just came down to say good-bye to Mollie.

MOLLIE. (*Crosses to* EMMETT; *a bit patronizing.*) Emmett, that's so dear.

EMMETT. Er—er—I wasn't sure you'd be glad to see me.

(FRANK *takes a great interest in the conversation.*)

MOLLIE. But of course I'm glad to see you. What makes you think that?

ANNE. (*She takes in the situation.*) Frank— (*Gestures him away.*) I want Mollie to take a Dramamine before she gets on the plane. Let's go find a Coke machine. Come on, Liz. (*They start off.* EMMETT *is gazing at Mollie, a woebegone look on his face.* FRANK *looks back curiously.*)

FRANK. I know my mind isn't attuned to subtleties, but are they—? (*Stops.*)

ANNE. It's all on his side. He's a terribly bright boy, really quite desirable, but he's a year younger. ,

LIZ. Three months.

ANNE. Well, he's a year behind her at school, so it's quite impossible. (*Pulls* LIZ.)

FRANK. Why? (ANNE *and* LIZ *look at him as if he has lost his mind.*)

LIZ. Daddy! When she's a sophomore at college—he'll be a *freshman!* It's just not done.

(*They are out.* MOLLIE *shakes her head at Emmett.*)

MOLLIE. Emmett, will you please take that look off your face. I can't stop *living.* (*Puts coat and magazines down.*) I have to go on with my life.

EMMETT. I can't help what I feel. I brought you something. (*He holds out a slender volume. She takes it.*)

MOLLIE. "Sonnets from the Portuguese." Oh, thank you, Emmett. I just love them.

EMMETT. (*Dead earnest.*) Elizabeth Barrett Browning

was six years older than Robert Browning. (MOLLIE *turns away.*) Need I say more?

MOLLIE. No.

EMMETT. And Beatrice Webb was older than Sidney Webb. And Martha Washington had a year on George!

MOLLIE. (*Turns to* EMMETT.) Emmett, you're an absolute panic! You're the first person in the world who ever did research for a farewell scene.

EMMETT. Will you write to me?

MOLLIE. I won't make a promise that I might not keep.

EMMETT. (*Overcome.*) You mean you won't even *write?*

MOLLIE. Emmett, you're a brilliant boy. But it's wrong. Why should I do anything to prolong a relationship that's doomed?

EMMETT. All right. I can see how much all of this means to you right now. But mark my words—however much you say "no," however much time and distance separate us—one day you'll realize this is inevitable! Have a good time. (*He starts off Left, comes right back.*)

MOLLIE. Thank you, Emmett. Good-bye. (*She holds out her hand. He takes it.*)

EMMETT. Good-bye. (*She leans forward as if to kiss him on the cheek. He pulls away; gestures.*) Please! None of your passionless kisses for me! (*He stalks off despondently.*)

(MOLLIE *looks after him a moment, a little sadly, but enjoying to some extent the emotional upheaval she has caused. A VOICE is heard over the loudspeaker.*)

LOUDSPEAKER VOICE. American Airlines Flight Thirty-Six now loading at Gate Seven. Passengers for American Airlines Flight Thirty-Six please report to Gate Seven.

(*In a moment,* FRANK, ANNE, *and* LIZ *rush back into scene.* ANNE *is carrying a Coke in a paper cup.*)

FRANK. Come on, Mollie. Your plane's loading. (*They start to collect Mollie's possessions.*)

ANNE. Here, darling, take a Dramamine. (MOLLIE *downs it.*) And leave some Coke. I want your father to take one, too. Here, Frank. (*She hands him a pill and he swallows it with the remains of Mollie's drink.*)

LIZ. What does that do?

FRANK. (*Tensely.*) It relaxes you! (*Then drinks— gives cup to* ANNE, *crosses to* MOLLIE.) Have we got everything?

MOLLIE. (*Counting quickly.*) Two coats, one bag, cookies, dressing case, two books, magazines—that's eight.

FRANK. Eight.

MOLLIE. I'm only supposed to have seven.

FRANK. Seven.

MOLLIE. (*Remembers.*) Oh, yes. Emmett gave me a book.

FRANK. Your ticket?

MOLLIE. Right here.

FRANK. (*Picks up large bag.*) Let's go. There's no turning back now.

(*They* ALL *go toward Left proscenium, laden down with Mollie's possessions. They do a Left turn, and come right back on again. As they do this, the arrival and departure sign disappears. In its place is a steel link fence with a booth at the end, labeled "Gate 7." A* MAN *in an American Airlines uniform is taking tickets from imaginary passengers, stamping them, and waving the passengers through.* MOLLIE *and her* FAMILY *get on the end of the imaginary line, gradually moving step by step toward the gate.* FRANK *is the center of the group. They talk across him and jostle him as they move. The AIRPLANE NOISES are louder, and a WIND is blowing. Everybody speaks in a shriek in order to be heard.*)

ANNE. I thought Emmett came to see you off. What happened to him?

MOLLIE. (*Screaming back at her mother over the noise.*) Poor boy. I'm afraid I was mean to him.

ANNE. Maybe we should save him for Liz.

LIZ. (*A very high-pitched shriek.*) Thanks, but I'll find my own. Cast-off dresses, yes; cast-off men, go home!

ANNE. Well anyway, Mollie, I wish you'd been nicer to him.

MOLLIE. Mother, you can't be nice to Emmett. He's too domineering. And to be dominated by a child— Well, anyway, I don't see the point to this whole discussion. It's all part of my past.

FRANK. (*He has been reacting to this feminine chatter with an expression of distaste. Finally raises his voice louder than anybody's.*) Please! I love you all very dearly, but constantly being surrounded by women and listening to their—

MOLLIE. Daddy, you'll be surrounded by one less from now on.

FRANK. (*He is silent for a moment. MOLLIE isn't even gone yet and already he misses her. AIRPLANE NOISE has grown softer.*) Yeah. That's right. You'll remember what I told you, Mollie?

MOLLIE. Daddy, you've told me many things and I remember all of them.

ANNE. Your ticket.

(ALL *watch as* MOLLIE'S *ticket is validated.*)

FRANK. Well, good-bye. (*They kiss. Then ANNE and* LIZ *kiss her too.*)

ANNE. 'Bye, darling.

MOLLIE. 'Bye, Mom. (ANNE *gives her coat and dressing case. To* LIZ.) 'Bye, Kook. (LIZ *gives her cookies and magazines.*)

LIZ. 'Bye, Mol'.

(*Almost completely obscured by her possessions,* MOLLIE *goes through the gate.* LIZ *and* ANNE *move back and wave farewells.* FRANK *stands, completely unaware*

that he is still carrying Mollie's large bag. MOLLIE
hurries to the fence.)

MOLLIE. (*Hissing.*) Daddy! (FRANK *looks at her.*)
Daddy! The bag!

(FRANK *looks down at bag, then looks nervously at the*
TICKET TAKER, *who continues about his business.*
Concealing the bag as best he can, FRANK *sidles to*
Left side of fence, hands the bag over, and manages
to hook it onto MOLLIE'S *arm. Practically hidden*
under the load, MOLLIE *turns and scuttles toward*
the plane. FRANK *takes a deep breath, and then*
walks out of playing area to Left proscenium.)

FRANK. That's the first criminal act I ever committed
in my entire lifetime! But, as I said, she has a fine mind
and I *did* ask her to use it. (*The steel link fence dis-*
appears, as at Stage Right the MICHAELSON LIVING
ROOM rolls in. ANNE *is at the drink set-up Downstage*
extreme Right, fixing a drink.) Later that night, I thought
to myself—I must be crazy. (*He moves into living room*
area and talks to ANNE.) What are we doing, taking one
of our dearest possessions, encasing it in a missile, and
hurling it from one end of the country to the other?
ANNE. Shall I fix you one, too?
FRANK. Thanks. Suppose all she comes back with is
a husband? There are plenty of those around here. California's full of boys. *And* colleges. (*Sits on couch.*)
ANNE. You're absolutely right. There's no law that
says she has to marry somebody from the Ivy League.
(*She hands* FRANK *his drink.*)
FRANK. I can see this is going to be a tough four years.
(*Holds up his glass.*) Well, to Mollie. (ANNE *echoes his*
words, and BOTH *drink.*)
ANNE. (*Thoughtfully, as she sits beside him.*) She's not
going to miss us at all.
FRANK. (*Reciting a set speech.*) I know. That means
we've done a good job. She's well-adjusted. She doesn't

care if she never sees us again. God, what a lot of psychological crap is thrust on the world these days!

ANNE. (*After a pause.*) Frank, I think we should take up a hobby— This didn't just pop into my head. I've been thinking about us—Mollie at home was a very big part of my life and your life. I don't think we'd have made it without her and Liz.

FRANK. Aaah, there was never anybody for me but you, and vice versa.

ANNE. A lot of people who love each other don't make it. But that has nothing to do with the fact that you are hopelessly, uncritically, head-over-heels in love with your daughters. And for the greater part of the next four years one of those two shining faces won't be here to greet you every night. That's why I think we ought to find something to do together. Something we could do at night.

FRANK. Are you about to make an indecent proposal?

ANNE. (*Smiles.*) Oh, I wasn't going to give *that* up. This is something else. (*A pause.*) I think we should go to Arthur Murray's.

FRANK. Arthur Murray's? (*Looks at her as if she's insane.*) What on earth for? I don't need dancing lessons. I'm the best dancer in my age group.

ANNE. You never dance Spanish rhythms. I think we should go to Arthur Murray's and learn Spanish rhythms.

FRANK. Annie, do you suppose I want too much for Mollie? I mean, suppose she comes back too smart? A misfit? Somebody who makes the boys feel inferior? I don't want her left on the vine.

ANNE. (*Puts glass down.*) Mollie won't be left on the vine. Now, what about Arthur Murray?

FRANK. (*Doesn't hear that—wrapped in his own thoughts. Gets up and walks Downstage.*) You know, it's a form of torture.

ANNE. What?

FRANK. Well—the way a daughter gets hold of you. (*Trying to make her understand.*) It's—it's like adoring some beautiful woman who—just tolerates you.

ANNE. (*Rises, puts arm on* FRANK'S *shoulder.*) Mollie

doesn't just tolerate you. She treats you that way because she's absolutely confident of your love. It's no problem. She knows you're never going to fall in love with anybody else's daughter. (FRANK *still broods.*) My God, she's only been gone three hours and you're so—so Hamlet! You'll never make it to Christmas. Now what about Arthur Murray?

FRANK. I don't have to go the whole four years she's in college, do I? (*They embrace and the LIGHTS go out in the living room.*)

(*MOLLIE'S ROOM at the Dorm at college appears Stage Left. It is night, and MOLLIE is in robe and pajamas, finishing a letter. The main lighting is supplied by a desk lamp, and only a small part of the room is visible. MOLLIE pulls the letter out of the typewriter and signs, speaking as she does so.*)

MOLLIE. "Love, Mollie." (*Reading what she had already written.*) "P.S. I'm the only one in my class still wearing a retainer on her teeth. It's not the kind of thing I care to be individual about. Please ask Dr. Schick if it's essential. If he says yes, I shall probably lose it. P.P.S. I heard Norman Thomas speak last Monday night on disarmament, which he naturally regards as absolutely necessary, and isn't the world situation just abysmal? Sometimes I think it won't last another week—and here I am still a virgin." (*She had apparently run out of space on the P.S.'s and had written around the margins, making it necessary for her to turn the letter as she reads. She puts letter down and starts to address envelope.*)

(*LIGHTS APPEAR again in the MICHAELSON LIVING ROOM. FRANK, in slacks and sport shirt, comes into room, picks up chair, holds it over his head, and starts to practice the rhumba, counting to himself. The purpose of the chair is to keep his shoulders from moving. He goes slowly across the room, shifting his weight cautiously from one foot to the other*)

LIZ *comes down the steps and watches her father, mouth slightly open.*)

LIZ. What the hell are you doing, Daddy?

FRANK. (*Lowers chair.*) I'm practicing the rhumba.

ANNE. (*Enters with small bowl of fruit and clean ashtray. To* LIZ.) And watch your language.

LIZ. The rhumba?

FRANK. (*Without stopping his workout.*) You see, the rhumba has anthropological roots. It didn't begin as a dance.

LIZ. (*Moves Downstage Right, to watch.*) It's not ending as one, either.

FRANK. (*Imperturbably.*) Nevertheless, its cultural origins derive from the native carriers moving through the jungle in Africa. This chair represents the burdens they carried on their heads. As they walked, they had to *feel* their way. They couldn't look down. Often the footing was treacherous— (*He reaches one foot forward cautiously to demonstrate.*) Then, having found firm ground, they shifted their weight and moved with the other foot. (*He moves his weight to the forward foot, achieving an accompanying hip gyration, and extends his other foot.*) Did you get that hip movement?

LIZ. That the way they teach the rhumba at Arthur Murray's?

FRANK. I'm getting special attention. The instructor has taken a fancy to me.

LIZ. She has?

FRANK. *He* has. (*He and* ANNE *laugh.*) Well, your mother thought I ought to have a hobby, and this is it.

LIZ. The mailman. (*She runs off.*)

FRANK. Hey, Annie, do you remember how you're supposed to turn? (*He tries to turn around, gets hopelessly tangled in his own feet.*)

ANNE. Take a rest, Frank. Let that chair become a chair again. (*He puts the chair back.* LIZ *returns, a packet of letters in her hands. She riffles through them.*)

LIZ. Letter from Mollie!

ANNE. How wonderful.

FRANK. (*Simultaneously, taking the letter and tearing it open.*) It's about time.

(*He settles himself beside* ANNE *on couch.* LIZ *sits on hassock. She and* ANNE *wait expectantly. After a moment, it is quite obvious that he has completely forgotten about them, and is absorbed in the letter.*)

ANNE. Read the letter, darling.

FRANK. (*He comes to with a start, and reads.*) "Dear Family, this is the first chance I've had to write. For days now I've been oriented, registered, examined—by the way, I have poor posture, but so does everyone else apparently —indexed, filed, everything but fingerprinted. I've even had my diction analyzed, and for some reason it came out New Jersey. Can you explain that?"

ANNE. That's ridiculous. She's never been east of the Mississippi.

LIZ. (*Rises and crosses to sofa.*) You were born in New York, Daddy. She probably caught it from you.

FRANK. What's wrong with her speech, anyway? What's the matter with those people?

ANNE. They didn't say anything was wrong with her speech. They just said it was New Jersey. Will you go on with the letter?

FRANK. (*Reading.*) "But enough of that. Our room is just fabulous, now that Adele and I have it decorated. We went into town and got some secondhand Degas prints for practically nothing. But best of all, borrowed a fabulous bullfight poster from her sister, who is not a student here, but guess what? The Registrar of the college! So Adele not only knows all the customs and traditions of this place, but all the rules and regulations as well. It's practically like living with a chaperone. Daddy, you couldn't have done better if you'd picked her out yourself."

(FRANK *is looking very pleased. Through that, the MICHAELSON LIVING ROOM has gone off, and*

DORMITORY comes on. MOLLIE *and her room-mate, a darling-looking girl named* ADELE MC-DOUGALL, *are surveying with satisfaction the results of their decorating, which runs to checked bedspreads and a large bullfight poster over one of the beds.)*

ADELE. (*On bed.*) I think we're a couple of damn geniuses. (*Hops up on other bed and adjusts poster.*) Maybe we ought to go in for interior decorating.

MOLLIE. (*Rises.*) It's absolutely fabulous. Everything! (*Looks out window.*) The campus is just beautiful. As a matter of fact, the only thing wrong with Hawthorne College for Women—is that there are no men.

ADELE. (*Taps the side of her head sagely.*) Now I can see why you got fifteen-o-four on the College Boards. Right to the heart of the matter.

MOLLIE. Well, how do you get to meet some? Is there a system? I mean, do we sign up some place?

ADELE. (*Comfortably.*) Oh, they find you. They have the same needs you do. Right now, two Gung-ho freshmen at Dartmouth are trying to figure out how to get down here and attack you and me.

(*At that moment,* SARAH WALKER *wanders into their room.* SARAH *is about the same age as the other girls, but is ever so much more sophisticated. She wears the same kind of clothes they do, but hers always look a little better. She is quite stunning. She carries a cigarette in a long holder.)*

SARAH. (*In doorway.*) This place is a goddam *nunnery.* (*She takes a long drag at cigarette and paces across the room.*)

MOLLIE. Oh, hello, Sarah. You talking about the same thing we are?

SARAH. (*To* ADELE.) To whom? Did you see what I drew for a roommate? (*Turns her eyes up to heaven.*) Quel horreur, mes enfants! (*Puffs cigarette, turns back to audience. Looks around the room at the prints and posters.*) Your room looks like a dream. You know what the decor of our dump is? Gold cups! She's got a gold cup for tennis, swimming, basketball. I've got my toothbrush in a gold cup for Sportsmanship! (*Sits on bed.*)

MOLLIE. Sarah, what are you doing in college, anyway?

SARAH. It's all my mother's idea. She's been married seven or eight times, and every once in a while she gets a spasm that I'm being neglected. My presence here is the result of one of those spasms. Actually, parents are idiots. They don't know, and I'm certainly not going to tell them, but kids whose parents are divorced get twice as much attention as the other kind. (*Looks out window and stands transfixed.*) My God! Men! (MOLLIE *and* ADELE *turn as one and stare out window, both demanding to know "Where?"*) Getting out of that car. (*Crosses to* ADELE.) They're from Hah-vad.

MOLLIE. How can you tell?

SARAH. There's no sticker on the windshield. Imagine! They drove all the way from Harvard! That blond one's cute.

MOLLIE. What are they doing here?

ADELE. They've come to look over the new crop.

MOLLIE. Us?

ADELE. Who else? They sort of prowl around and ear-mark what they like for future reference. Shall we? (*Opens door.*)

SARAH. Certainly. Coming, Mollie?

MOLLIE. It's perfectly revolting. (*Turns to look out window; doesn't see* ADELE *and* SARAH *exit Left.*) Do you girls really plan to go parading out there to be looked over like prize pigs at the Pomona Fair? Why, I would no more do anything like that than— (*Turns and realizes Adele and Sarah are gone.*) Where is everybody? (*Scrambles over bed, looks down hall. Then she looks out window again. After a moment, she smooths her hair and runs out after the other girls.*)

(*DORMITORY disappears, and Stage Center, the*

CAMPUS FENCE comes on. Three boys are leaning against it, surveying the passing scene. They are the blond, good-looking one named DONN BOWDRY, *who is a junior and very wise; a small chunky freshman who will be called* 1ST FRESHMAN; *and a burly, athletic type who will be called* 2ND FRESHMAN.)

DONN. All in all, this is our best bet. It's close enough so you don't have to pay for hotel rooms on week ends, and they come in the same shapes and with the same accessories you'll find at any other institution of learning.

1ST FRESHMAN. How cooperative are they?

DONN. Well, don't try to make it on the first date. The American female finds that insulting. On the other hand, I understand from some guy who was on a Fulbright last year that European women——

1ST FRESHMAN. (*Sees imaginary girl. Gestures to* DONN.) Hey, take a look at that.

DONN. Hi! Glad to see you back. (*With their eyes, the* BOYS *appreciatively follow her progress across the stage, Left to Right. When she has gone,* 1ST FRESHMAN *looks questioningly at* DONN. *He shakes his head.*) Junior. Pinned. M.I.T. Madly in love. Sea-green incorruptible. Our game is freshmen. (*They nod sagely to indicate their mature understanding.*)

1ST FRESHMAN. (*Pointing.*) That one looks nice. The one in the checked pants.

DONN. (*After a look.*) My dear boy, she's an absolute pig.

1ST FRESHMAN. Listen, I'm no beauty myself. Who wants to go out with a girl who's so damn gorgeous she thinks she's doing you a favor?

DONN. (*Gazing raptly off Left.*) Wow! Take a look. (*The other two look also.*)

2ND FRESHMAN. Are they new?

DONN. (*Without taking his eyes off the* GIRLS.) I never saw them before—and if I never see the tall one again, I'll kill myself.

(SARAH *and* ADELE *come on Left, and walk demurely past the* BOYS. *The* BOYS *watch with admiration as the* GIRLS *go by, not hurrying their pace. As soon as they have gone by the boys,* SARAH *stops.*)

SARAH. (*Offering her pack.*) Cigarette, *Adele?*
ADELE. Thank you, *Sarah.*

(*Slowly,* SARAH *lights* ADELE'S *cigarette and her own.* MOLLIE *comes rushing on from Left; as soon as she sees the* BOYS, *she slows down, and joins her friends.*)

SARAH. No need to rush, *Mollie.* I'm just going to post a letter.

(SARAH *and* ADELE *proceed off Right.* MOLLIE *takes a backward look at the* BOYS, *and follows. The* BOYS *watch their every movement.*)

2ND FRESHMAN. Well? What do we do now? Just stand here?
DONN. (*Nods calmly.*) Mmmhmmm. You heard her. She's just going to post a letter. There's no mail box down there—and there *is* one right in the dorm. (*Very sure of himself.*) They'll be back.

(Two OTHER BOYS *come on up* R. *They are upper classmen, typical collegiate types named* RICHARD GLUCK *and* ALFRED GREIFFINGER.)

RICHARD. Hey, Harvard, anything good around?
DONN. Dogs, nothing but dogs. (*Elaborately.*) So dismal we're contemplating doing our military service this year.
1ST FRESHMAN. Yeah. As soon as we get back to town, we're enlisting.
RICHARD. (*Catches on quick.*) Oh. Found something good, huh?
DONN. Yeah. But let's not spoil it with a snow job, shall we?

(RICHARD *looks off Stage Right. The* GIRLS *are evidently returning and he reacts with proper reverence.*)

RICHARD. Ma-ma Mia! (*The* GIRLS *are near enough to be recognized.*) Hey! That's Mollie Michaelson! (*All excited.*) Went to high school with me. Two years behind me. Boy, she's grown up! (*The* GIRLS *are on now.*) Mollie!

MOLLIE. (*Peers at him a moment.*) Richard! Richard Gluck! (*Runs; they embrace like old friends.*) Somebody told me you were at M.I.T. (*They break away and smile at each other.*) Oh, girls, I want you to meet Richard Gluck. (SARAH *and* ADELE *join* MOLLIE.) Richard, this is my roommate, Adele McDougall, and another friend of mine, Sarah Walker.

(*They exchange how-do-you-do's as all the* BOYS *make mental notes of the names.*)

RICHARD. And this is a classmate of mine, Alfred Greiffinger.

(*Another exchange of greetings.* DONN *and his chums line up, ready to be presented.* RICHARD *turns his back on them pointedly.*)

SARAH. (*A half-whisper.*) Mollie— (*Indicates the other* BOYS; *she has had her eye on* DONN.)
MOLLIE. (*Nods.*) Richard, who are they?
RICHARD. I don't know. Think they run a kennel in town, or something. Come on, let's all go have some coffee. (*Links arms with* MOLLIE *and starts off Left.*) All freshmen? (SARAH *following, with* ADELE *and* GREIFFINGER.)
SARAH. Mmmmhmmm. Untouched by human hands.

(*They are out, leaving* DONN *and his two despondent friends behind.*)

1ST FRESHMAN. Well? I thought you were going to kill yourself?

Donn. Not me. Sarah Walker, Mollie Michaelson, and Adele—

2ND Freshman. (*Supplies the name, wistfully.*) Mc-Dougall.

Donn. (*Nods.*) There's a lot of time ahead of us, a long, cold winter, and the time of the singing of birds will come.

(*The CAMPUS FENCE and the* Boys *have gone off through that, and action starts again in the MI-CHAELSON LIVING ROOM, where* Frank *is finishing the letter as* Anne *and* Liz *listen.*)

Frank. "So Friday night I went out with Richard Gluck, and Saturday night I went out with a fraternity brother of his who is a junior named Alfred Greiffinger, who took me to dinner and a lecture by Margaret Mead, who said that young people at college should not marry, but should experiment." (*Looks at* Anne.)

Anne. Who said that? Margaret Mead or Greiffinger?

Frank. (*Studies letter.*) Apparently Margaret Mead, because— (*Continues to read.*) "I was under the impression that she meant experiment mentally, but later on I found out he thought physically, and since we reacted so differently, I don't think I'll be seeing much of Alfred Greiffinger any more." (*Sigh of relief.*) "Anyway, this Friday it's Richard Gluck again, and Saturday Adele has dated me with a Williams boy from her home town who she says is utterly obnoxious." (*Laughs.*) "But *anything* is better than being without a date on Saturday night. I know this probably sounds awful to you, but that is an accepted fact in this female society of which I have now become a member, and I haven't been here long enough to start being a non-conformist, nor have I any desire to. I have signed up for English, French, Biology and Modern European History. Two of my instructors are crocks—" (Liz *laughs.* Frank *evidently doesn't see anything amusing.*) "but my History professor is fabulous. Oh, by the way, we've put in our own telephone, Maple

62984." (ANNE *writes number down on pad.*) "Love, Mollie." There's a P.S. (*He follows Mollie's handwriting up the side of the page.*) She doesn't want to wear her retainer. And P.P.S. (*Reads slowly, deciphering the writing.*) "I heard Norman Thomas speak last Monday night on disarmament, which he naturally regards as absolutely necessary, and isn't the world situation just abysmal? Sometimes I think it won't last another week—and . . . here I am—still a—" (FRANK's *voice trails off. He puts the letter down, folds it over and hands it to* ANNE, *a thoroughly disillusioned man.*)

ANNE. (*She rereads the letter from the beginning, with relish.*) I think it's marvelous. Or should I say fabulous?

FRANK. What's fabulous about it? They're handing her around like a hot potato.

ANNE. This is the time for her to be handed around. And Mollie can take care of herself. You saw the way she managed that Greiffinger person. She won't get into trouble.

FRANK. (*Gets up.*) I didn't send her three thousand miles just not to get into trouble! (*Strides toward telephone.*) I'm going to call her.

ANNE. (*Blocks him off.*) No, Frank, no! Don't call her when you're angry. Wait till tonight when you've cooled off and the rates are down. (FRANK *sits.*) Come on. (ANNE *tries to pull* FRANK *to his feet.*) Let's practice your rhumba.

FRANK. (*Refuses to get up.*) No, Annie, no. Anyway, I can only do it with a chair on my head. I can see myself for years at parties—every time they put on a rhumba, I pick up a chair! Pretty soon people will stop inviting us. We'll sit here alone, night after night. We'll take to drink. All because you said we ought to go to Arthur Murray's! That was a terrible thing to do, Annie.

(*Through that, MICHAELSON LIVING ROOM has disappeared. DORMITORY ROOM now appears Stage Left.* MOLLIE *and* ADELE *are studying.* MOLLIE *is on the bed, reading from a thick literary tome.*

ADELE *is sketching a diagram with great concentration. Both* GIRLS *are in pajamas and robes.*)

MOLLIE. (*Reading.*)
"When in disgrace with fortune and men's eyes,
   I all alone beweep my outcast state,
   And trouble deaf heaven with my bootless cries,
   And look upon myself and curse my fate,
   Wish me to be like—"
ADELE. Mollie, please. I'm diagramming the inside of a
frog, and I put her pancreas where her stomach ought to
be. (*Sighs and starts to erase.*)
MOLLIE. (*She reads a little more and exhales ecstatically.*) How could I have got to be eighteen years old and
not realize how fabulous Shakespeare's sonnets are?
(*Phone rings.* MOLLIE *picks it up from floor.* ADELE *also
reaches, but too late.*) Hello?— (*Enthusiastically.*) Why,
hello, Alfred!
ADELE. Who? (ADELE *looks at her questioningly. She
covers mouthpiece and hisses.*)
MOLLIE. Greiffinger! (*Back to phone, sweetly.*) Oh, I'm
so sorry. I already have a date for next Saturday. Can I
have a rain check?—Good— (*Rises and crosses to desk
with phone.*) I'll look forward to hearing from you.
(*Hangs up; puts phone on desk.*)
ADELE. Whom you going with next Saturday?
MOLLIE. (*Flops on her stomach on bed, face to audience.*) Nobody. (*Back to Shakespeare.*)
"Let me not to the marriage of true minds admit
   impediment.
Love is not love which alters when it alteration
   findeth—"
   (*Puts book down and looks at* ADELE, *seriously.*)
Do you suppose this is all a waste? I mean, let's face it,
woman's real purpose in life is marriage, children, propagate the species, and all that stuff. Does it make you any
more desirable as a wife because you know the meaning
of a Shakespeare sonnet, or you can describe intimately
the inner workings of a female frog?

ADELE. I intend to keep it a secret. Might scare somebody away. How many articles have you read on the aggressive American female?

MOLLIE. Exactly. But if they teach us all this stuff, aren't we supposed to use it? And if we use it, does that make us aggressive?

(SARAH, *also in robe and pajamas, enters and yells back into corridor.*)

SARAH. Well, if you don't like it, go to the goddam house mother and tell her I smoke cigars and you want a new roommate. (SARAH *slams door and sits on edge of* ADELE'S *bed. Now utterly charming to* MOLLIE *and* ADELE.) Listen, mes amies, I have a weekend date at Yale, and he has a friend. (*Looks from one to the other.*) Now, who's available? Before you snap at this golden opportunity, I want to warn you—he's short.

ADELE. I have no problem—I'm planning to defend my honor in Dartmouth this weekend.

SARAH. Dartmouth? (*Shrugs.*) Many have tried—few have succeeded. (*To* MOLLIE.) Anyway, that narrows the field considerably.

MOLLIE. (*Warily.*) How short is he?

SARAH. Five-two. (*Hastily.*) But what the hell? It's a chance to see Yale, we'd be together, and who knows what you might meet down there.

MOLLIE. Yeah, but—

SARAH. Come on, Mollie. Listen, my mother's happiest marriage was the shortest—in height, I mean.

MOLLIE. Okay. But this is a week-end date. I'll need a letter of permission. There isn't time to write—

SARAH. Why don't you wire?

MOLLIE. Yes. I could do that. What's his name?

SARAH. (*Rises.*) Stanley Underdown. (MOLLIE *and* ADELE *stare at her.*) I can't help it.

MOLLIE. And short, too. They're always the hardest to handle. Always trying to *prove* something.

(*The PHONE RINGS*—ADELE *picks it up.*)

ADELE. Hello? Yes, she's here. Mollie, long distance. (MOLLIE *scrambles over bed and grabs phone.*)

(*The MICHAELSON LIVING ROOM comes to life in response.* FRANK *is on the phone, with* ANNE *hovering to get the sound of Mollie's voice.*)

MOLLIE. Hello!

FRANK. (*His anger evaporates like magic. He is beaming.*) Hello, Mollie. How are you, sweetie?

MOLLIE. I'm just fine, Daddy. Wonderful to talk to you. How are you and Mom and Liz?

FRANK. Fine. I'm glad I found you in. How's college?

MOLLIE. Just wonderful.

FRANK. What are you doing?

MOLLIE. I'm right in the middle of a paper on the sonnets of Shakespeare. Isn't Shakespeare fabulous, Daddy?

FRANK. (*To* ANNE.) Shakespeare is fabulous, too.

MOLLIE. What?

FRANK. Nothing, darling.

MOLLIE. Is there something wrong, Daddy?

FRANK. No, no.

MOLLIE. You're sure everything's all right?

FRANK. Yes, yes. I just wanted to talk to you—

MOLLIE. (*Sits on bed.*) Well, it's marvelous that you did, because I have this wonderful invitation to go to New Haven for the week-end, but I need your permission. So will you please write a letter to my house mother, her name is Miss Helen Pickett, with two "t's," and say that it's all right for me to spend the week-end at Yale as the guest of Stanley Underdown?

FRANK. Who? Do I know him?

MOLLIE. Of course not. I don't even know him myself. I'm being fixed up.

FRANK. (*Appalled.*) You're being what?

SARAH. (*She gets up and crosses to* MOLLIE.) He lives in the same house that Averell Harriman lived in.

MOLLIE. He lives in the same house as Averell Harriman.

FRANK. Averell Harriman! Are you going out with him?

MOLLIE. Of course not.

ANNE. (*All excited.*) What about Averell Harriman?

FRANK. I don't understand a damn word of this.

MOLLIE. Never mind. Just write it. You also have to say you understand that suitable housing will be arranged and you absolve Hawthorne College of all responsibility for me on the week-end. Daddy, will you please get that in the mail tonight?

FRANK. I'll do nothing of the kind!

(MOLLIE *rises, paces.*)

ANNE. What? What?

FRANK. She wants to spend the week-end at Yale, suitably housed with some unknown character named Stanley Underdown!

ANNE. How perfectly marvelous. Give me that. (*Takes phone.*) Mollie, dear, it's Mom. Now tell me exactly what I have to do. (*Making notes.*)

MOLLIE. (*Sits on bed.*) Hi, Mom! Wonderful to talk to you. Now, all you have to do is write a letter to my house mother, Miss Helen Pickett, with two "t's"—

ANNE. (*Noting the name.*) Yes, dear. What else?

MOLLIE. And say that I have your permission to go to Yale—

ANNE. Yale! How wonderful, darling!

MOLLIE. As the guest of Stanley Underdown, spell it just the way it sounds—

ANNE. (*Busily writing.*) It sounds dreadful, dear, but I will—

(*As* MOLLIE *signals an "okay" to* SARAH, *both MI-CHAELSON LIVING ROOM and DORMITORY*

*disappear and the stage now represents the STREET
OUTSIDE MICHAELSON HOME. There is a
representational mail box, extreme Left. EMMETT is
Stage Center, listening to CHAMBER MUSIC on a
small transistor which he holds to his ear, and gazing
up at Mollie's window. After a moment, FRANK
appears, a letter in his hand. There is a bemused
expression on his face. He walks right past EMMETT
without seeing him, on his way to mail box.)*

EMMETT. Hello, Mr. Michaelson.

FRANK. Hello— (*Peers at him in the darkness.*) Who's
that? Oh, Arnold!

EMMETT. It's Emmett, Mr. Michaelson.

FRANK. (*Suddenly* EMMETT *looks good to him.*) Oh,
Emmett! Emmett, I'm so glad to see you. (*Shake hands.*)

EMMETT. How's Mollie? Have you heard from her?

FRANK. Yes. As a matter of fact, I just talked to her
on the phone a little while ago.

EMMETT. I don't suppose she mentioned me?

FRANK. (*Carefully.*) Well, she asked how everybody
was, so I suppose you could—

EMMETT. (*Dolefully.*) Mmm-hmmm.

FRANK. (*A keen look at him.*) Having a bad time?

EMMETT. Well— (*Turns front; quotes, philosophically.*) "Men have died and worms have eaten them—but
not for love." I'll survive. I suppose you'll think it's
stupid, but you know what I'm doing here? (*Looks
down.*) Every once in a while I just come over and stand
across the street and look up at her window.

FRANK. My boy, forget her. You've lost her, I've lost
her, we've both lost her. (*Brandishes the letter.*) Shall I
tell you what's in this letter? Permission for her to spend
the week-end at Yale with a total stranger!

EMMETT. (*Bristling with outrage.*) Well, do you think
that's right?

FRANK. I don't. I most certainly do not. I fought
against it like a tiger. But she's got permission, and I
signed it.

EMMETT. (*After a moment's thought.*) Mr. Michaelson, why don't you let me mail the letter for you?

FRANK. Oh, no. I thought of that. I have to live with these people— (*Starts off Left; sighs heavily.*) Fathers of sons have a much easier time of it.

EMMETT. Mr. Michaelson, I'm going to tell you something. You've got nothing to worry about with Mollie. (*Crosses to* FRANK.) Why, I once spent three hours on the top of Mulholland Drive trying to talk her into— (*Breaks off, confused.*) Well, what I mean is—

FRANK. (*Wrathfully, as he backs* EMMETT *across the Stage.*) I know exactly what you mean! (*Then, philosophically.*) Well—East, West—I can see that geography has nothing to do with it. I might as well put this in the mail. Good night, Arnold.

EMMETT. (*Starts to correct him, decides it's not worth while.*) Good night, Mr. Michaelson.

(*They go in opposite directions.* FRANK *drops letter in mail box, then comes down to proscenium Stage Left and talks to the audience.*)

FRANK. I don't know why I took it so big, because hot on the heels of Stanley Underdown came Adam Bassington, from Dartmouth; Leland Mendez, Princeton; Darcy MacNamara, Holy Cross; Johann Sebastian Vogel, Brandeis—and they all got permission to spend the week-end with Mollie and Hawthorne College was absolved of all responsibility. And then one day we got a letter saying, "He doesn't know it yet, but I have met a boy from Harvard who's going to marry me." That's all. That one didn't even have a name. (*The LIGHTS DIM on* FRANK *as he exits.*)

(*LIGHTS COME UP STAGE RIGHT to show* MOLLIE *dancing with* DONN BOWDRY, *the blond Harvard junior we met previously.* ADELE *is seated at a restaurant table, Stage Center, with a most intellectual and argumentative young man named* ALEX LOOMIS. *They appear to be not speaking. Both work on the lobsters on the table before them and watch the dancing. MUSIC DIM.)*

MOLLIE. Well, I'm having a marvelous time, but I think we ought to go back to the table.

DONN. Oh? Why?

MOLLIE. He's my date and there's no reason why Adele should be stuck with him.

(DONN *shrugs, and they go back to the table.* ALEX *makes a half-hearted attempt to rise, then slumps back as* MOLLIE *is seated.*)

DONN. Adele? Dance?

ADELE. Love to. (*They go to dance floor.* MOLLIE *starts on her lobster. She exchanges a frosty smile with* ALEX *and watches the dancing wistfully.*)

ALEX. It never fails.

MOLLIE. (*Coming to with a start.*) What?

ALEX. I said it never fails. Every time I double with Donn, my so-called "date" spends the entire evening admiring him.

MOLLIE. I wasn't admiring him. I was looking at him and Adele dancing. Is there anything wrong with that?

ALEX. No. Go ahead. Watch them dance.

MOLLIE. I'm sorry, Alex. We could talk, if you like.

ALEX. It's risky but I'm perfectly willing. What shall we talk about? How about One World?

MOLLIE. (*A deep breath.*) All right, Alex. Do you believe in One World?

ALEX. Do you?

MOLLIE. Yes. Do you?

ALEX. No, I don't.

MOLLIE. Why not?

ALEX. When something comes along that everybody believes in, you have to examine it very carefully.

MOLLIE. Then you're against it.

ALEX. Oh, I'm not against everybody having a place

in the sun. There's no stopping that. But the corollary notion that all people are equal is obviously ridiculous. (*Expanding.*) There will always be people of superior intelligence. In every tribal group, some people are born smarter than other people. There's no point to providing equal opportunity for everybody. Those who are better equipped should have better opportunity. (*A pause for breath.*)

MOLLIE. I see. What speech would you have made if I'd said I didn't believe in One World?

ALEX. (*Looks at* MOLLIE *keenly.*) That's very astute of you. I didn't think you were that bright.

MOLLIE. (*Miffed.*) I'm not. A dull-normal could tell that about you. (*Digs into her lobster, determined to enjoy something.*) This lobster is delicious. How's yours?

ALEX. All right. (*Unable to agree about anything.*) But if you'd ever had lobster on a beach in Maine, cooked over hot rocks and covered with seaweed—

MOLLIE. Well, I haven't! I'm from Southern California and this tastes great!

ALEX. Tell me, is Southern California really the intellectual desert everybody says it is?

MOLLIE. (*Restrains herself a moment, then.*) Certainly. Why, before I came East, I thought Marcel Prowst was some kind of new hairdo. (*Purposely mispronounced.*)

ALEX. Oh— (*He's very young.*) By the way, it's Proust.

MOLLIE. Really? You learn something new here every day, don't you? It's so stimulating.

(ADELE *and* DONN *re-enter.*)

ADELE. But she looks perfectly miserable; she looks as if she's going to break a plate over his head any minute.

DONN. It has happened. A Vassar girl.

ADELE. A Vassar girl? They're so isolated I'd thought they'd stand for anything. (*Indicates she'd like him to dance with* MOLLIE.) I'll go powder my nose.

(*He nods.* ADELE *goes and* DONN *goes to the table where* MOLLIE *and* ALEX *are eating in dogged silence.*)

DONN. Mollie—would you like to—? (*Indicates dance floor.*)

MOLLIE. (*Half out of her seat.*) Would I! (*Remembers her manners.*) You don't mind, do you, Alex?

ALEX. But you're right in the middle of your lobster. Aren't you going to finish it?

MOLLIE. No, no. I've had enough.

ALEX. Maybe I should get the waiter to keep it hot for you—

MOLLIE. (*Going off with* DONN.) Don't bother with the waiter. You just *talk* to it! (DONN *takes her in his arms and they dance off together.* ALEX *settles back in his place, very disgruntled.*)

DONN. Sorry if you're not having a very good time.

MOLLIE. Oh, that's all right. Is your friend on the debating team?

DONN. Organized activity? Alex? He might take on the whole team, he'd never join it.

MOLLIE. I've had some tough dates, but he and I are the mis-match of the century.

DONN. You know something, Mollie? I think so, too. We can't do anything about it tonight, but you and I are a much more interesting combination.

(ADELE *re-enters.* ALEX *doesn't see her. She holds back of her chair, lifts it, thumps it smartly on the floor and sits.* ALEX *stands up belatedly, knocks his chair over.*)

ALEX. (*Picking up chair.*) Terribly sorry. I'm not used to being out in civilized society.

ADELE. Perfectly all right.

ALEX. (*Directly.*) I don't suppose you want to dance, do you?

ADELE. How can I resist such a charming invitation? (*They go out onto dance floor.* ALEX *takes her in his arms, and they dance together, perfectly smoothly, gracefully.* ADELE *looks up at him in surprise.* MOLLIE, *dancing with* DONN, *turns in time to catch* ALEX'S *performance, and also registers surprise.* ALEX *goes into a deep dip with* ALELE, *and they dance off Right.*)

MOLLIE. That is the most unpredictable human being I have ever met in my whole life!

DONN. Forget him. Look, Mollie, I don't usually work this fast, but we might not be alone together the rest of the time. So, what are you doing next Saturday?

MOLLIE. (*Pulls away.*) I don't know.

DONN. Of course you do. And what about the Saturday after that?

MOLLIE. Am I being snowed?

DONN. I wouldn't use a line on you. That's so dull. I just want to see you Saturday, and the Saturday after that, and the Saturday after that——

MOLLIE. That's a pretty good line. But I like it. (*She and* DONN *dance off Left, as restaurant setup disappears.*)

(*MICHAELSON LIVING ROOM rolls on from Right. At Left end of couch, a small easel has been set up, holding a canvas with its back to audience.* FRANK *is on the opposite end of the couch, holding palette and brushes, as he lines up with his thumb the effect he wants to achieve on the canvas. He gets up and starts to paint, with great concentration, what appears to be a series of straight lines.* ANNE *comes in, carrying some sewing, and looks pleased to see him at work.*)

ANNE. Wouldn't it be extraordinary if you turned out to have talent?

FRANK. (*Painting.*) Not particularly.

ANNE. (*Looks at painting.*) What are you——doing this time?

FRANK. I'm painting us a Mondrian.

ANNE. Oh!

FRANK. Got my inspiration from the linoleum in the kitchen. (*He stops in the middle of a bold stroke.*) Isn't it about time we heard from Mollie?

ANNE. (*Crosses and sits on sofa.*) How often did you write home when you were at college? Mollie's in love. She's happy.

FRANK. Donn! Donn! Donn! What do we know about this boy, actually?

ANNE. Well, Mollie wrote about his family. They're wealthy, they live in New York . . .

FRANK. And they spend most of their time traveling in Europe! I don't like that.

ANNE. (*Astonished.*) What do you mean, you don't like that? What's wrong with traveling in Europe?

FRANK. He just doesn't sound right for Mollie. Sounds like everything's being handed to him on a gold plate.

ANNE. Oh, I know what you want. You want a boy who comes from Scranton, Pennsylvania, and they dragged him up out of a mine, gave him a scholarship, and shipped him off to Harvard!

FRANK. (*In complete accord.*) Yeah. Why doesn't Mollie find someone like that?

ANNE. You're going to discriminate against people just because they're wealthy? What kind of snob are you?

FRANK. (*Trying a new tack.*) Well, anyway, isn't Mollie a little young to have decided on one boy? I mean you went with lots of boys before I came along. You shopped around a little.

ANNE. Frank, last month you were complaining bitterly because she was dating too many boys. You said she was being handed around like a hot potato. You didn't like that.

FRANK. (*Firmly.*) No, I didn't.

ANNE. Don't you like it better now that she's only dating Donn?

FRANK. (*Just as firmly.*) No, I don't.

ANNE. I give up. (*She starts off.* FRANK *tosses his palette angrily on the couch, takes up a large yardstick, holds it against the canvas—it extends over the top by a foot and a half—and paints a straight line, using the stick as a guide.* ANNE *watches, as he turns the yardstick and paints another line at right angles to it.*) Oh, I think that's cheating.

FRANK. (*Imperturably.*) Mondrian has his methods, I have mine.

(*LIGHTS OUT in MICHAELSON LIVING ROOM. LIGHT COMES ON extreme Left, to show a CAMPUS BENCH.* ALEX *and* SARAH *are seated on the wall, in close embrace. Their dialogue consists chiefly of "Yes" from* ALEX, *and "No" from* SARAH. ALEX *moves in even closer and tries to hook his leg around her. She pushes him away suddenly.*)

SARAH. Stop it, Alex, stop it!

ALEX. Ah, come on. (*He lunges.*)

SARAH. For heaven's sake, take it easy. You'll knock out my contact lenses!

ALEX. (*Deflates.*) Oh, God! (SARAH *searches in her purse for her compact.*) Have you ever used that line before?

SARAH. (*Complacently.*) Mmmhmmm. (*Moves under light and finds comb, lipstick and compact.*) It sure knocks the hell out of romance, doesn't it?

ALEX. Who says it has to be romantic?

SARAH. Well, I'm just as avant-garde as the next one, but there must be some pretense. You can't even *pretend* your heart is in it. (*Looks at herself in the mirror and starts to repair the damage.*) You know, Alex, you're really quite sweet.

ALEX. What a bitchy thing to say.

SARAH. Oh, no. You are, and I intend to tell Mollie I found you fascinating.

ALEX. Resistible, but fascinating.

SARAH. Oh, practically everybody's resistible.

ALEX. Aaaah—I've given up on Mollie. She's being snowed by the champ. Donn is a kind of male Marilyn Monroe.

SARAH. He's quite the operator. Have you seen Mollie lately? (*Puts things back in purse.*)

ALEX. No.

SARAH. Mmmm—Très élégante, mon ami—I think she and Donn—

ALEX. I don't want to hear about them. The hell with sex. I'm giving it up for New Year's.

SARAH. And it isn't even Christmas yet. (*Rests her head on his shoulder.*) Joyeux Noël, Alex.

ALEX. (*Elegantly.*) Ap-cray!

SARAH. Well, it's been a delightful evening. (*She gets up.* ALEX *doesn't move, gazes gloomily ahead.*) Don't bother seeing me to my door. (*She goes.*)

ALEX. (*He sits a moment in silence.*) Oh, hell!

(*LIGHTS OUT on BENCH. Then the STREET OUT-SIDE MICHAELSON HOME appears. It is night. In a moment,* FRANK *walks on, Stage Right, from the direction of the house. It is winter, and he wears a heavy carcoat.*)

FRANK. Well, today is the day. (*Grins amiably.*) Mollie's coming home. Just called the airport. The plane's only forty-five minutes late. (*Sighs with anticipation.*) This is the longest she's ever been away from us— (*Ticks off on his fingers.*) September, October, November, December— And I still can't do the rhumba—I wonder if *she* learned anything. (*Shrugs.*) I don't really care. I just want to see her.

(ANNE *comes out to join him, followed by* LIZ. *Both wear coats.*)

ANNE. Frank, I called the airport again. The plane's on time.

FRANK. It is? (*Consults his watch.*) Those damn airlines. Do they know what they're doing? (*He brushes past them, and out.*)

LIZ. Mother, I think you'd better drive! (ANNE *nods and they follow.*)

(*There is the sound of a JET ENGINE screaming in for a landing. This in turn becomes the sound of the CAR ENGINE. DOOR SLAM is heard.*)

(*Through this, the MICHAELSON LIVING ROOM has rolled on, Stage Right. No one is on Stage, but the LAMPS are lit and the Christmas season is evidenced by a Christmas mobile in a corner of the room and various gift-wrapped parcels. LIZ's voice can be heard, babbling away offstage Right. None of her words should be understandable until her entrance.*)

LIZ. Be careful getting out of the car–– And the football team is an absolute disaster this year. After five games they finally scored a touchdown, and there was so much cheering it was positively humiliating. Of course, football isn't important, but still— (*In course of this, ANNE comes in first, looking distraught. She takes off her coat, drops it on Upstage chair, and turns toward door. FRANK follows her in. He is stunned. He carries Mollie's large bag, walks with it to far end of couch, drops it on floor, and also turns toward door. LIZ now comes in, also carrying some of Mollie's possessions.*) Everyone is dying to see you. The phone's been ringing all day.

(MOLLIE *comes in, and takes a long look around at the room. The cause for shock is quite apparent. She is wearing a sophisticated black coat and dress; long earrings dangle just above her shoulders; her hair is arranged in a bubble cut, or whatever else is the latest; she puffs inexpertly at a cigarette in a long holder. The* FAMILY *studies her.*)

MOLLIE. (*Finally.*) I've been thinking about this moment for weeks. (*Another pause to look around.* ANNE *comes Downstage for a closer look at her. She still doesn't believe it.*) It seems so much smaller. Have you done something to it?

ANNE. Oh, no, dear, I don't think so.

MOLLIE. Everybody says there's nothing very Christmassy about Southern California—but I *feel* very Christmassy. (*Drags on cigarette, as she turns to face her father.* FRANK *sits suddenly on sofa.* MOLLIE *notices the sunk look on his face and goes to him.*) What's the matter, Daddy?

FRANK. I don't know. Except maybe—just to keep pace—I should have raised a little beard while you were gone.

ANNE. Darling, did you have a good sleep on the plane?

MOLLIE. (*Crosses to* ANNE.) No. As a matter of fact, I didn't sleep at all.

ANNE. Oh— But I thought— Your hair—

MOLLIE. (*Bristling slightly.*) What about my hair?

ANNE. Well, nothing, nothing. I just didn't realize you do it that way deliberately.

MOLLIE. I *knew* you wouldn't like it. (*Appeals to* FRANK.) Do you, Daddy?

FRANK. I'm not sure. I have to get used to it first.

MOLLIE. *Donn* is crazy about it.

LIZ. I like it. I wonder how it would look on me—

ANNE. Shut up.

MOLLIE. Well, now that the initial shock of seeing me is over—may I have a martini, please? Very dry?

FRANK. No! (*Gets up.*) Not even very wet!

MOLLIE. (*Crosses to* FRANK.) Daddy, that's perfectly ridiculous. I drink on dates. What do you want me to do? Smoke behind the fence?

FRANK. (*A look at* ANNE. *She shrugs helplessly.*) Oh, all right. (*He starts toward drink set-up.*)

MOLLIE. What kind of gin do you use?

FRANK. (*Takes, just a bit.*) My own label! I've been making it in the cellar for years! (ANNE *takes* FRANK's *coat and he starts to mix drinks.*)

MOLLIE. Donn says House of Lords is the only gin.

FRANK. Really? And what vermouth?

MOLLIE. Noilly Prat, of course.

FRANK. (*Stirs drinks.*) Outside of a bartender, what's Donn studying to be?

MOLLIE. Oh, Daddy, they *all* have to go into the service first. But after that, he's planning to be an international tycoon, or some such.

ANNE. Some such?

MOLLIE. They *all* want to make money.

FRANK. (*Pouring drink.*) Well, there's nothing wrong with that. (*He hands* MOLLIE *her drink.*)

MOLLIE. (*Holds her drink.* EVERYBODY *watches to see what she'll do with it.*) Isn't anybody going to drink with me?

FRANK. Certainly. (*Holds martini pitcher to his mouth.*)

ANNE. Frank!

FRANK. Oh, all right. (*He pours for himself and Anne. Addresses* LIZ *with mock politeness.*) What about you, Liz? (*Gestures invitingly with glass and pitcher.*)

LIZ. (*Grandly.*) Since you haven't got House of Lords, I'm not interested.

FRANK. (*Sits on hassock with drink.*) Well, what's college like, Mollie? Is it all it's cracked up to be?

MOLLIE. (*Crosses to* FRANK.) I'm on cloud seven, Daddy. I can't wait to get back.

FRANK. (*Miffed.*) Thanks.

MOLLIE. (*Kneels beside him.*) Oh, I don't mean it that way. Of course I love all of you— (*Stands up.*) But aside from that—what is there for me here? I've outgrown all my friends.

FRANK. They didn't just stand still. They got older, too.

MOLLIE. (*Patiently. Crosses Left Center.*) Daddy, there's just something about the *East.* It's—well, it's the *East.*

FRANK. I'll go along with that.

MOLLIE. (*Sits sofa, Left end, puts drink down.*) Do you know that out of sixteen Rhodes scholars chosen from all over the United States—seven came from Harvard?

ANNE. (*Sits on hassock beside* FRANK.) I think that's very interesting, don't you, Frank?

FRANK. No. Not particularly. I wasn't asking about Harvard. I was asking about Hawthorne College for Women.

MOLLIE. Don't you see? It's all part of the same intellectual climate.

FRANK. Oh. Are you planning to be the first woman Rhodes scholar?

MOLLIE. Not a chance. Not me. I'm just about skinning through.

FRANK. (*Gets up, crosses to* MOLLIE, *shocked*.) You're kidding!

MOLLIE. (*Quite calmly*.) I am not. You might just as well make up your mind to it. (*Rattles off her words quickly, this has all been thought out long ago*.) The only way you can get honors at Hawthorne is by being an absolute grind. You've got to work all the time and turn down dates. And if you do, people look at you as if you're absolutely queer or something. It's really an awful rat-race. If you *don't* go out every week-end, you feel rejected; and if you *do* go out, you have this terrible sense of guilt. After all, is that what you came to college for? The girls and I talked it all over. (*Philosophically*.) The only solution is to fall in love and have all the pressures removed. (*They all stare at her for a moment*.)

FRANK. (*Finally*.) How?

MOLLIE. It's very simple. That way you know exactly what you're doing every week-end, so you don't spend any time thinking about it.

FRANK. (*On hassock*.) Oh!

MOLLIE. (*Gets up*.) Well, I guess I ought to unpack.

ANNE. (*A little fuddled*.) Yes. If you're staying.

(MOLLIE *looks at* ANNE. ALL *go toward bags*. MOLLIE *starts to pick up the big one*.)

FRANK. I'll take that up for you, dear. (*Takes bag and goes upstairs*.)

MOLLIE. Thanks, Daddy. (*She and* LIZ *gather up the rest of her possessions and start upstairs after* FRANK. *To* LIZ, *as they go.*) How are things at good old Beverly High?

LIZ. About the same. Joan Shockworth had to leave school.

MOLLIE. No!

LIZ. Well, you don't put on ten pounds in two months just by over-eating—

(ANNE *is alone. She contemplates her martini seriously, puts her hand to her forehead. After a moment,* FRANK *returns.*)

FRANK. Now don't worry about it, Annie. It's just a stage.

ANNE. I'm not worried.

FRANK. Well, don't. She'll get over it. (*Reassuring himself.*) It's—it's Hegelian. (*Paces.*) Thesis, antithesis, synthesis. She'll be better off as a result. (*Sits beside* ANNE.)

ANNE. Well, I don't know how Hegel got into it, but I wish you wouldn't take it so seriously. It's really kind of funny. You send off what you think is going to be the first woman President of the United States—and you get back Betty Boop!

FRANK. (*Gets up and crosses room.*) Yes. You're absolutely right. It's not life or death. It's just a passing phase.

ANNE. Exactly. Take a look at that martini. She didn't have more than a sip.

FRANK. (That's true. (*He has it.*) Helps to take the pressure off. (*There is the sound of a CAR DOOR SLAM from outside.* FRANK *looks out the window.*) Somebody in this house is getting flowers.

ANNE. What?

FRANK. There's a florist's truck just out—- (*DOOR-BELL rings.* ANNE *rises. Puts glass down on table.*) I'll get it. (*He throws the door open to reveal* EMMETT.

EMMETT *carries an extraordinary basket of flowers in which roses rub shoulders companionably with chrysanthemums and carnations, and daisies. The colors are not very compatible.)*

EMMETT. Good evening, Mr. Michaelson. (*Comes in, sets flowers on floor in front of couch.)*

FRANK. Well, for heaven's sake, it's—er— (*Looks to* ANNE *for help.*)

ANNE. Emmett.

EMMETT. Good evening, Mrs. Michaelson.

ANNE. How nice to see you, Emmett.

FRANK. What *are* you?

EMMETT. Christmas job. I need every cent I can lay my hands on this Christmas. Is Mollie home?

FRANK. She's here. (*Calling.* EMMETT *puts hat on sofa.*) Mollie! Mollie!

MOLLIE'S VOICE. Yes, Daddy?

FRANK. (*Yelling back.*) Emmett's here!

MOLLIE'S VOICE. Hi, Emmett! I'll be right down.

EMMETT. Hi, Mollie!

FRANK. Annie, why don't we drive out to Santa Monica and pick out a Christmas tree?

ANNE. Sounds exciting.

FRANK. This year let's get a white tree with gold balls.

ANNE. (*Horrified.*) What on earth for?

FRANK. Oh, I don't know. It's just so *West.*

(EMMETT *picks up book.*)

ANNE. (*Laughs.*) All right. Just let me check and see if we need anything else in town. (*She goes.*)

EMMETT. I see you're reading "The Rise and Fall of the Third Reich."

FRANK. Mmmhmmm.

EMMETT. (*A considered opinion.*) I found it—quite superficial.

FRANK. You did?

EMMETT. I think perhaps that's because we're too close

to that event to be able to evaluate it properly. Don't you think so, sir?

FRANK. Errr— (*He is saved by* MOLLIE'S *appearance.*) Aaah! Here's Mollie.

EMMETT. (*Puts book down.*) Hello, Mollie.

MOLLIE. (*Extends hand.*) Emmett—

(FRANK *sits on hassock.*)

EMMETT. Here. (*He moves the flower basket in front of* MOLLIE.) For you.

MOLLIE. Oh, they're lovely, Emmett. But you shouldn't have spent so much—

EMMETT. What's the difference? It's the sentiment, isn't it?

(FRANK *makes a great show of not listening.*)

MOLLIE. Yes. But they look so expensive.

EMMETT. (*Candidly.*) Oh. They weren't expensive at all. I'm working for a florist this Christmas—and I took one flower out of each bunch.

MOLLIE. (*Crosses, a little cool.*) I see.

EMMETT. How are you, Mollie? Gee, I have a million things to say to you. (MOLLIE *nods.*) What about riding around Bel Air on the truck with me while I make my deliveries?

MOLLIE. I'd love to, Emmett, but I just got off the plane and I didn't have five minutes sleep last night— (*Sits on sofa.*)

EMMETT. (*Sits beside her.*) You look just fine to me, Mollie. (*Heartily. Points to hair.*) Just comb your hair and come on.

(FRANK *looks pained for* EMMETT.)

MOLLIE. (*Ice cold now.*) What?

EMMETT. (Nothing *gets through to him.*) Then just come on. Nobody's going to see you, anyway.

MOLLIE. I don't know how you manage, Emmett, but you have a positive genius for putting things in such a way—

EMMETT. (*Astonished.*) What are you talking about? What did I say? (*Rises. Appeals to* FRANK.) Did I say anything, Mr. Michaelson?

FRANK. I— (FRANK *looks at him. How can he tell him briefly, tersely, the workings of the female mind? Finally, just gestures helplessly with both hands.*)

MOLLIE. Thank you for the flowers, Emmett, and thank you for the invitation, but I'm completely exhausted.

EMMETT. Oh? Okay. (*Moves flowers to* MOLLIE.) Gee, Mollie— (*Picks up hat.*) this isn't the way I wanted it to happen. I've been thinking about this for months.

MOLLIE. It's all right, Emmett. Really it is. I'll see you.

EMMETT. (*Considers this an opening.*) What are you doing a week from tonight?

(FRANK *has given up all pretense of not listening. Watches with fascination.*)

MOLLIE. A week from tonight?

EMMETT. (*Quickly.*) You couldn't possibly have a date. You just got here.

MOLLIE. (*Resigned.*) All right. I couldn't possibly have a date. What did you have in mind?

EMMETT. (*Sits on sofa. Inventing—not too skillfully.*) Well, there's this—my uncle and aunt are here from Denver—and they're throwing this big party at the Beverly Hilton Hotel for my jerk cousin—who's transferring to U.C.L.A.

MOLLIE. Oh.

EMMETT. (*Hastily. A deep breath.*) First we have to go to their suite and have cocktails.

MOLLIE. All right. Is it formal?

EMMETT. No, no. Very *in*formal.

MOLLIE. At the Beverly Hilton? Are you sure, Emmett?

EMMETT. Positive. I'm in charge of all the arrangements. (*Rises. Crosses to door.*) See you Friday. (*He is out.*)

MOLLIE. (*Gestures dramatictlly in the direction of the departed Emmett.*) There! Do I have to submit any more evidence to prove my case?

FRANK. Case? What case are you talking about?

MOLLIE. People just take a longer time to mature in the West, that's all.

FRANK. (*Rises. Crosses to* MOLLIE.) Oh, Mollie, the kid's just trying too hard. He's working like a dog trying to impress you. (*Puts flowers Upstage.*) He's been counting the days until you got home. The minutes, judging by the way he popped in here. (*She softens a little.* FRANK *sits on sofa.*) Why do you suppose he's driving that florist's truck? (*Pleading Emmett's case earnestly.*) He wants to make money so he can spend it all on you! You'll probably have a great time Friday night. He's bright, he's interesting. Of course when he's with you, he acts like an absolute idiot. He's so smitten, all the wrong words come out of his mouth. But if you give him half a chance—

MOLLIE. (*Kisses* FRANK's *hand.*) All right, Daddy, all right. (*Gets up.*)

FRANK. I have a hunch about him, Mollie. He's going to be somebody.

(LIZ *comes in.*)

LIZ. What did the creep want?

MOLLIE. (*Shrugs, goes toward stairs.*) Oh, he's taking me to some party at the Beverly Hilton. I really don't want to go, but I'd hate to have people out here thinking of me as a snob. (*She is gone.*)

(FRANK *and* LIZ *look after her for a moment.*)

FRANK. (*Resolutely.*) I won't think of her as a snob.

I don't know what I *will* think of her as, but I won't think of her as a snob.

LIZ. (*Crosses to* FRANK *and hugs him.*) Oh, Daddy! You're such a dreamer!

(*The LIGHTS are OUT in the MICHAELSON LIVING ROOM. A DRESSING TABLE appears Left Center. Its back is to the audience and* ANNE *is seated at it, peering through the mirrorless frame of the table at the audience. She is in evening clothes and is evidently planning to attend a Bal de Tête, for she is making the final adjustments to a small papier-mache Christmas tree which she has fixed on her head. It is quite becoming.* LIZ's *voice is heard from Offstage.*)

LIZ's VOICE. Where are you, Mom?
ANNE. I'm upstairs, dear.

(*She adjusts a pin in her headdress. In a moment,* LIZ *comes in, dressed for bowling, holding a star made of aluminum foil.* NOTE: *This is a quick change for* LIZ *and should be achieved by the addition of a simple accessory, like a sweater, added to last scene's costume.*)

LIZ. (*Holds out star.*) See, Mother. It worked. Out of aluminum foil. Look how nice that star came out.

ANNE. Well, aren't you smart? Thank you, darling.

LIZ. (*She fixes it on top of headdress arrangement.*) You know they can't miss having a fight.

ANNE. Who?

LIZ. Mollie and Emmett. Did you see the way she greeted him? (*Very snooty, imitating Mollie.*) "How *are* you this evening, Emmett?"

ANNE. (*A slight smile.*) Patience, Liz, patience.

LIZ. What ever happened to "Hi, Emmett"?

ANNE. Liz, she'll never again be as old as she is right now. Not if she lives to be a hundred. What time will you be home?

Liz. Well—bowling—then everybody's bound to be hungry— Oh, about twelve.

Anne. No later.

Liz. I'm doubling, Mother, so I'll just have to do the best I can. (*There is the sound of a HORN HONK from outside.*) Oh, God! I wish I were old enough to go with someone who rings the doorbell instead of honking! (*The HONK is repeated.*) Night, Mom. (*Kisses her* Mother, *calls as she runs off.*) Night, Daddy.

Frank. Night, sweetie! (*He comes in, only partly dressed in his preparations for a black-tie party. He finishes his dressing on Stage, taking in* Anne's *headgear.*) Hey. I had no idea you were going to be that elaborate.

Anne. (*Working away on her appearance.*) I hadn't planned to, but Millie Crowder has been working on hers for a week. She's got a whole Chinese village on her head. (*Makes a final adjustment and rises.*) There! (Frank *says nothing, too busy with himself in the mirror.*) Well, for heaven's sake, say if you like it or not. Do you realize how much work I—

Frank. (*Hastily.*) I'm mad about it. I might even vote for you, if you're terribly nice to me afterward. (*Kiss.*)

Anne. Oh, sure.

Frank. (*He nods and studies himself in mirror, as he completes dressing.*) You know, when my father was my age, I used to think he was old. But I feel kind of snappy tonight.

Anne. (*Gets up.*) Now sit down and I'll do you.

Frank. (*Appalled.*) Wait a minute. If you think I'm going to put something like that on my—

Anne. (*Pushes him into seat.*) I worked out something very simple. (*She picks up a Turkish towel.*) If people are giving a "bal de tête," everybody has to go along with it or it's no fun.

Frank. (*Suspiciously.*) What am I going to be?

Anne. A sheik.

Frank. (*Looks at himself in mirror.*) With that face? (*Makes a grimace.*)

ANNE. (*Calmly, adjusting headgear.*) You're a member of a different tribe from Rudolph Valentino.

FRANK. The ugly tribe.

ANNE. Now hold still.

FRANK. (*He looks up at her.*) Annie, you look beautiful. (*Holds her around the waist a moment.*)

ANNE. Thank you.

FRANK. (*Turns to mirror again.*) And didn't Mollie look pretty tonight?

ANNE. Mmmhmmm— (*She is tying a cord around the towel, to try to get the proper effect.*)

FRANK. And Emmett—I almost didn't recognize him. He really looked—well— (*Can't go too far.*) bearable.

ANNE. (*Completes her work.*) There! How do you like it? (*Looks at* FRANK.)

FRANK. (*He studies himself in the mirror from various angles. Flatly.*) I look exactly like a man with a towel on his head. (*They both look up sharply as* MOLLIE'S VOICE *is heard from downstairs.*)

MOLLIE'S VOICE. Daddy! Mom! (FRANK *and* ANNE *exchange a puzzled look.*)

FRANK. Mollie? What's she doing home?

MOLLIE'S VOICE. Would you come down please?

ANNE. Something's wrong!

(FRANK *and* ANNE *both run off Right. LIGHTS ALL OUT. MICHAELSON LIVING ROOM rolls on in darkness.* WHITMYER *is heard talking on the telephone.*)

WHITMYER. Yes, dear. Everything's under control—Angel, stop worrying. I took care of everything— She's all right. He's all right— (*By now, the LIGHTS are on in the living room, to reveal* MOLLIE, EMMETT, *and Emmett's father,* MR. WHITMYER, *talking into the phone.* MOLLIE *and* EMMETT *are both in party attire.* MOLLIE *is at the foot of the steps, looks furious.* EMMETT, *very hangdog, stands beside his father.* MR. WHITMYER *is a small, energetic man whose face is very red just now.*

No, no. No police, and nothing will be in the newspapers— Of course he's all right— I'll let you talk to him. (*Holds out phone to* EMMETT *but doesn't let go of it.*) Here! Say hello to your mother!

EMMETT. (*Weakly, into mouthpiece.*) Hello, I'm—

WHITMYER. (*Puts phone back to ear.*) Your precious little darlins is fine, see? We'll be home right away. (MR. WHITMYER *hangs up as* ANNE *and* FRANK *are seen coming down the steps.*)

MOLLIE. Mother and Daddy, I want you to meet Mr. Whitmyer. (*Points to* EMMETT.) That monster's father!

(FRANK *and* ANNE *move forward and say nothing, waiting for a clue.*)

WHITMYER. How do you do? (*To* EMMETT, *sternly.*) You're going to apologize to Mr. and Mrs. Michaelson, and then I'm going to take you home and— (*Breaks off.*) I wish you weren't too big to thrash! (*Pushes* EMMETT *roughly to a position between* FRANK *and himself.*)

EMMETT. (*A mumble.*) I apologize.

FRANK. What for?

WHITMYER. Go on! Tell these decent people what for?

EMMETT. I apologize for— (*Stops short.*) I can't say it! (*Turns his back and stumbles to a position behind his* FATHER.)

MOLLIE. Well I can! He apologizes for trying to attack me in the Beverly Hilton Hotel!

FRANK. What?!

MOLLIE. That party with his cousins from Denver! They don't exist! He made it all up! He and I were the only ones at the party! He rented the room! (*Sits on sofa. A look at her* FATHER.) And you said I wasn't being nice to Emmett. I was being too tough. Well, next time he wants a date, *you* go with him!

FRANK. Well, he's not too big for me to thrash!

(*Starts after* EMMETT. EMMETT *uses his* FATHER *as a shield and retreats Stage Right,* WHITMYER *getting*

mauled by him and FRANK *in the process, as* ANNE
gets in the middle.)

ANNE. (*Holding* FRANK *back.*) Frank, Mollie said he
only *tried*. Nothing happened.

WHITMYER. Fortunately. Fortunately for all of us the
assistant manager of the hotel is a friend of mine.

FRANK. I don't see anything fortunate about anything
in this whole business!

WHITMYER. (*He retreats.*) Well, anyway, they were
seen going up in the elevator. This manager friend of
mine had the house detective bring them down to his
office. And instead of calling the police, he called me.
Tell them what name you registered under!

EMMETT. (*Very small.*) John Keats.

WHITMYER. (*Stands between* MOLLIE *and* EMMETT.)
Mr. and Mrs. John Keats! See? No ordinary boy. You
and your goddam poetry! (*Pushes* EMMETT. EMMETT
falls down. Back to FRANK *and* ANNE.) Number one in
his class. Straight A's. (*Crosses up.*) Already admitted to
four colleges, including Harvard—

MOLLIE. Oh, no!

WHITMYER. (*Riding through.*) And this is what he
uses his genius for! (*Very abject. Crosses down.*) I
couldn't be more sorry. We've all known about Mollie for
years. Emmett's told us how brilliant and wonderful she
is— (*Sees* EMMETT, *still on the floor.*) Stand up, boy.
(EMMETT *gets to his feet.*) Lucky that man was a friend
of mine or we'd all be at the police station right now.
(*Looks at* FRANK *across room, takes in headdress for the
first time.*) Have you got a headache?

FRANK. What? (*After a moment, he remembers.*) Oh,
for God's sake! I forgot all about this. (*He pulls the
towel off his head, makes a ball of it, and flings it at*
ANNE, *as if she were somehow at fault.*)

ANNE. (*Crosses to* EMMETT.) Emmett, how could you?
I mean, all the years you've been coming to our house.
How could you?

EMMETT. (*On the verge of tears.*) Mrs. Michaelson.

you know how I love Mollie. And—well—Mr. Michaelson told me she's been getting permission to spend week-ends— (FRANK *looks around.*) at Dartmouth with other guys—and Yale, too— (ANNE *and* MOLLIE *both look at* FRANK, *surprised.*) and I just wanted to prove I'm as good as they are.

FRANK. (*Cutting him off.*) If I were you, Emmett, I'd shut up about what I was trying to prove!

EMMETT. But Mollie still thinks of me as a little kid, and I'm just as—

WHITMYER. (*Also cutting him off.*) Mr. Michaelson is right. Shut up, boy! It's the smart ones who cause all the trouble.

FRANK. Mr. Whitmyer, do me a favor, take him away. Please take him away, because if I ever get my hands on him, you're going to have a son entering Forest Lawn—not Harvard!

WHITMYER. (*Pushes* EMMETT *toward door.*) Go on, son. I'm going to take him home, and tomorrow morning, I'm going to sell his car!

EMMETT. Oh, Dad! (*They are out.*)

FRANK. And I used to feel sorry for the little bastard—standing across the street looking up at your window. Mollie, I must apologize. Apparently, I'm responsible for your having a thoroughly humiliating experience.

MOLLIE. Oh, I'm not really marred. Takes more than that to mar me. (*Rises.*) In some ways it was kind of funny. (*Crosses.*) By the time I get back to school I'll reappraise it and it'll be a hilarious story to tell the girls. (*She sits on hassock.*)

FRANK. (*Crosses to* MOLLIE.) But I was so wrong—

MOLLIE. Of course you were. It isn't anything you know anything about. I may not have learned much scholastically, but I did learn about men. Some are safe and some are unsafe. Emmett is unsafe. (FRANK *looks very unhappy.*)

ANNE. (*Helpfully.*) It's important to learn about that, too, Frank. (*Hands* FRANK *the towel.*)

FRANK. (*Sunk.*) Of course. (*Looks at his watch.*) We'r

late for the party, huh? (*A look at* MOLLIE.) I—er—er—
is it all right to leave her alone?

MOLLIE. What are you going to do? Get a sitter for
me?

FRANK. I guess not. (*To* ANNE.) Coming? (ANNE
*nods, and goes toward stairs, stopping a moment to rest a
comforting hand on* MOLLIE's *shoulder. The PHONE
rings.* FRANK *picks it up.*) Hello?—Yes, she's here. Just
a moment. (*To* MOLLIE.) For you. Long distance.

(MOLLIE *hurries to take the phone, and* ANNE *continues
on upstairs for her wrap.*)

MOLLIE. (*Into phone.*) Hello?—Yes, this is she—
(*Her voice is suddenly warm and vibrant.*) Donn?—
(*Sits on sofa.*) Donn! How wonderful!—Are you having
a great vacation?—Oh?—(FRANK *crosses to bar, his
back to audience. World-weary.*) Yes, isn't it the truth—
Just about the same here— Oh, nothing very much,
except something awfully funny just happened. You'll
panic when I tell you about it. Absolute riot— You don't
know it, Donn, but you're involved with a femme fatale—
Mmmmmmmm—Mmmmmmmm— (*She giggles.*) Er—
er— (*Before she can look at* FRANK, *he realizes he is
eavesdropping and goes into hall.*) Well, of course, I miss
you too, darling. (FRANK *crosses hall and exits.*) Terribly— Oh, they're wonderful, but I don't even feel as if I
belong here any more. I just didn't realize how *provincial*
—It's really sort of sad— Oh?—Sounds marvelous—
(*Slowly.*) I don't know what my folks'll say—I'll ask.
They might— Well, I'll let you know in plenty of time—
Look, this is costing you a fortune. Good-bye, darling—
Of course I do— Good-bye— (*Hangs up.*)

(*After a moment,* FRANK *returns.*)

FRANK. (*Tentatively.*) How's—how's Donn?
MOLLIE. Oh, he's wonderful.
FRANK. So I gather. (*There is a pause.*)

MOLLIE. (*Also tentative.*) Daddy— (*Rises.*)

FRANK. Yes?

MOLLIE. Donn invited me to spend New Year's Eve in New York, and it would only mean leaving two or three days earlier— Would you and Mother mind? (*Looks at* FRANK.)

FRANK. (*Crosses to sofa. Sits. After a moment.*) I was under the impression you just got here.

MOLLIE. (*Sits.*) I've been here seven days already!

FRANK. (*Another moment to take it in.*) Seven whole days.

MOLLIE. Well I wouldn't be leaving till next week. And it's New Year's Eve in New York, and who is there for me to go out with here?

FRANK. Yes. That's very important.

MOLLIE. Oh! (*She looks upset. Turns away from him.*)

FRANK. I'm not being flip, Mollie. It's very depressing to stay home New Year's Eve. Almost as depressing as going out.

MOLLIE. Well then?

FRANK. (*Gives up.*) Why don't you take it up with your mother? (*Turns away.*) I don't feel entirely qualified. She's the one who gives permissions. Whatever you two decide. (*There is an awkward pause.*)

MOLLIE. What's the matter?

FRANK. Nothing. Nothing's the matter.

MOLLIE. (*Looks at* FRANK.) Oh, I can read you like a book. I could when I was four, and I still can. (*Looks front. A moment.*) You're terribly disappointed in me, aren't you? You expect me to be Eleanor Roosevelt or Madame Curie—and I'm not.

FRANK. (*Turns to* MOLLIE.) I don't want Madame Curie. I just want you to be the best you can.

MOLLIE. Has it occurred to you that this might be the best I can? And if that's so, what's wrong with it? Is it wrong to want to be liked and accepted?

FRANK. I'm not talking about conformity and non-conformity. I'm talking about you. And to see you *settle* for this— Yes, when I see what's important to you, I *am* disappointed.

MOLLIE. Daddy, I'm a perfectly ordinary girl. Why don't you face it?

FRANK. (*Very gently.*) Mollie, I've known you a long time. I know your potential. I know your capabilities. It's so much more than this. You know that, don't you?

MOLLIE. (*Shakes her head. Rises.*) Yes.

FRANK. Couldn't you give it another try?

MOLLIE. (*She softens, affected by the seriousness of his tone.*) I don't know what star you want me to reach for.

FRANK. Neither do I. But I know you have it in you to be something wonderful. You just have to work at it.

MOLLIE. (*After a moment.*) I'll try. (FRANK *gets up and comes to her.*) And I'll begin by spending New Year's Eve in California.

FRANK. That's my girl. (MOLLIE *throws her arms around her* FATHER's *neck. He holds her.*)

MOLLIE. Oh, Daddy! I'm never going to love anybody as much as you love me. It must hurt like hell!

(*As they stand in close embrace:*)

THE CURTAIN IS DOWN

END OF ACT I

ACT TWO

TIME: *Now.*

AT RISE: *As Curtain rises,* FRANK *is seen, Stage Right, leaning one arm on the telephone pole and looking out at the audience. He has the air of a man who has been through a great deal, and is engrossed in thought.*

FRANK. The first year is supposed to be the hardest—but I think that's only true of marriage. (*Sighs deeply.*) Anyway, we're now in our sophomore year, and Hawthorne College, having done such a brilliant job on Mollie the first year—as you saw—rewarded itself by raising the tuition. I complained bitterly to Annie—and mailed the check. (*Smiles wryly.*) Money doesn't stop us. We're determined to be educated. (*Changes, takes on the manner of an orator.*) We put behind us the bubble hair, the dry Martini, and the word "fabulous," and we moved into a new phase. We became socially conscious. (*Thinks about it for a moment.*) That was what I was pulling for all the time, but Mollie has a way of going all out that— (*Stops, shakes his head.*) For example, she marched up and down outside the British Consulate in Boston shouting "Free Bertrand Russell"; of course he'd been let out of jail two weeks before—but that really wasn't the point. She busted up her romance with Donn when she discovered he was for Barry Goldwater. She also spearheaded a drive demanding to know on what basis the faculty had turned down the drama club's decision to do "Lady Chatterley's Lover" as its attraction for the father-daughter week-end. This was resolved when the dean explained she thought the students were mature enough—but she wasn't so sure about the fathers. (*A pause.*) And then in the second half of her sophomore year, Mollie wrote us that she probably wouldn't be home

that summer. She had applied for a job with the State
Department to work overseas. (FRANK *beams. This he
approves of.*) She took a test, and in answer to the question, "Do you have any preference as to the kind of work
you will do or where you will be sent?" she answered,
"Anything, any place, as long as it helps the cause of
peace." (*His grin broadens.*) How about that?

(FRANK *disappears, and the LIGHTS COME UP on the
DORMITORY ROOM, Stage Left.* MOLLIE, *on desk
chair, and a lusty young female named* LINDA LEH-
MAN, *on the bed, are twanging their guitars with great
gusto.* SARAH *and* ADELE *sit on other bed.* ALL *are
singing "Tseiner." This is an Israeli song which is
played and sung with spirit and audience participa-
tion in the way of handclapping.* SARAH *and* ADELE
supply the handclapping. ALL *apparently have been
affected by the socially conscious phase, which is evidenced in an utter disregard for what they are wearing and what the hair fashion is that particular year.
Stark simplicity is the order of the day. "Tseiner"
comes to an end. They wind up with a flourish, out
of breath and fired with zeal.*)

MOLLIE. Oh, Linda! You're so lucky to be Jewish!
LINDA. (*Astonished.*) That's a switch. I always heard
it the other way round.
MOLLIE. Well, all the people we admire are Jewish.
SARAH. That's right, Mort Sahl, Sigmund Freud . . .
ADELE. Salinger— The New Yorker one, I mean.
MOLLIE. Adlai Stevenson!
LINDA. Who?
MOLLIE. Of course he's not, but he really is, if you
know what I mean.
SARAH. Certainly.
LINDA. Oh, you girls are absurd, the next thing you'll
want to spend your third year in Israel dancing the Hora.
SARAH. I'd love to. I find Jewish men fascinating.

(*Dreamily.*) Leonard Bernstein! He could conduct me any place.

LINDA. Oh, you're just picking isolated examples.

(*PHONE rings.* MOLLIE *picks it up.*)

MOLLIE. Shalom! Who's this? Oh, hi. This is Mollie. Linda's right here. (*Holds out phone to* LINDA.) Clancy Sussman.

LINDA. Yes, Clancy— You're kidding!—You signed the lease for the coffee house— Tremont Street! You'll be rolling in money— What are you going to call it? "The Manic Depressive"?—That sounds so commonplace— Certainly, Clancy, I'll be there opening night with my guitar clutched in my hot little hand-— Oh? Well, I'll ask her— Call you back— Good-bye, Mr. Sussman. (*Hangs up.*) Well, what do you know? Clancy's really going to open a coffee house.

SARAH. But Linda, how much can you make out of a coffee house? It's just coffee and—

LINDA. Oh, Clancy's putting in a full menu.

MOLLIE. Anything Clancy Sussman turns his hand to is bound to succeed. I just have that feeling about him. (*PHONE rings. She picks it up.*) Yes, who's speaking? (*Her voice turns to ice.*) No, Emmett, I will not fix you up with another girl! Not after your behavior last time! Jennifer was furious with me for having suggested you. Even by the loose standards around here, you're a sex maniac! Why don't you take up some reasonable vice, like—like dope—or alcohol—or—or boys? And do me a favor, Emmett: Lose my phone number! (*She bangs up the telephone.*)

ADELE. Well, you certainly chopped him.

LINDA. Mollie, how would you like to make seven dollars a night—twice a week? (MOLLIE *looks at her.*) Clancy has this brilliant idea of having folk singing every Friday and Saturday night. We're what Clancy calls "Ambiance."

MOLLIE. Ambiance? (*Still wary.*) What kind of songs will we sing?

LINDA. Oh, you know. Ballads and things. (LINDA *picks up guitar and plays and sings.*)

> "My father was hung for sheep stealing
> My mother was burned for a witch
> My sister's a bawdy house keeper
> And I'm a son of a—"

(*All the* GIRLS *join in here.*)

ALL (*Singing.*)
> "Fa-la-la-la-la-la Fa-la-la-la-la-la-
> Fa-la-la-la-la-la Fa-la-la-la-laaaaaaaaaa."

(*On the last syllable of the song, the DORMITORY is off, and MICHAELSON LIVING ROOM is on, with* FRANK *seated on the sofa, holding a letter, and* ANNE *beside him, consulting the dictionary.*)

ANNE. (*On sofa.*) Ambiance. Here it is. (*Reading.*) "Environment; surroundings; especially in decorative art. The totality of motifs or accessories surrounding and enhancing the central motif." (*She and* FRANK *exchange a puzzled look.*)

FRANK. She has the damnedest extra curricular activities I ever heard of. (*Returns to the letter as to something distasteful.*) "Clancy Sussman is really some kind of genius, not only in school but in the financial world as well. While every other night spot in town is half empty, The Sleeping Pill is always jammed—" (FRANK *looks at* ANNE.) "Except that is—not lately. The trouble is Clancy is quite mad and absolutely unpredictable. If Gerry Mulligan is in town he simply doesn't show up to open the place."

ANNE. Who's Gerry Mulligan?

FRANK. Baseball player.

ANNE. Oh!

FRANK. (*Continues letter.*) "I haven't heard yet on the

European deal for this summer but Adele's sister says they always take time. Everybody in my poetry class has developed a mad crush on our professor, but (ho-ho) he seems to have eyes only for me. I'm doing my term paper on T. S. Eliot and we've had really inspirational conferences about it. The campus gossip is that he's divorced and I wouldn't be surprised. He has such a hurt look about the eyes. Makes you want to take care of him. It will probably be the best thing I've ever done."

ANNE. What?

FRANK. The paper—I think.

ANNE. Well, does it say that?

FRANK. No, it just says it'll probably be the best thing she's ever done. Does everybody go through this?

ANNE. I guess so. It's the price you pay.

FRANK. For what?

ANNE. I don't know. You just pay it.

FRANK. "Anyway, folks, you know where I am every Friday and Saturday night. Daddy if you were planning to come for father-daughter week-end, you could hear us in person, but since you're not I've sent you a record we made so you'll know how we sound. Please make allowances for the acoustics. The Sleeping Pill used to be a bowling alley. Love, Mollie." Maybe I'd *better* go up there for father-daughter week-end.

ANNE. Oh, sure. Five hundred dollars to see your daughter for two days?

FRANK. (*Picks up small flat package and rises.*) Maybe it broke. (*Opens package as he crosses to record player.*) Nope. Not even a scratch. (*Puts record on.*) Well, bombs away. (*MUSIC ON. A horrible WAILING SOUND is heard. After a moment,* FRANK *turns machine off.*)

ANNE. Wrong speed. (*She fixes record player. The record is now playing at normal speed.*) You see? That's not *too* terrible. (*They both listen with enjoyment,* FRANK *even doing a little directing.*)

MOLLIE'S AND LINDA'S VOICES. (*On record.*)
"Here's to the girl who steals a kiss and stays to steal
    another,

Here's to the girl who steals a kiss and stays to steal
      another,
She's a joy to all mankind
She's a joy to all mankind
She's a joy to all mankind—
And she'll soon be a mother!"

(*They are both stunned for a moment, then* ANNE *gets
up and goes to* FRANK.)

ANNE. You go up there, Frank! I don't care what it
costs—you go up there!

(FRANK *nods his agreement, and LIVING ROOM DIS-
APPEARS. THE SLEEPING PILL comes on, Stage
Center, tables and chairs, dimly lit by CANDLE-
LIGHT.* LINDA *and* MOLLIE *are seated on high
stools, playing their guitars and singing "The Tat-
tooed Lady." They wear peasant dresses and strings
of beads.* CLANCY SUSSMAN *is seated at a table,
reading a book. Clancy is a tall, thin young man, who
slouches rather than walks. He looks as if he has
never had enough to eat.*)

LINDA AND MOLLIE. (*Singing.*)
           "I paid a dime to see
           The tattooed lady
           Tattooed from head to toe
           That's quite a sight you know
           And over on one thigh
           Was a British Man o' War."

CLANCY. (*Waving to an imaginary customer.*) Good
night Ed, come again.
LINDA AND MOLLIE.
               "And across her back
               Was a Union Jack
               Now who could ask for more

And up and down her spine
Ran the Mason-Dixon line
And in a certain spot
Oo—oo
Was a blue forget-me-not
And over on one kidney
Was a bird's eye view
Of Sidney
But what I like best
Right across her chest
Was my home in Tennessee."

(*They finish the number to a very thin spatter of applause, and take their bows very unprofessionally.*)

MOLLIE. I think there are six customers in here.

LINDA. I counted eight. (CLANCY *comes to them, applauding, though he is the only one.*) Are we doing better, Clancy?

CLANCY. (*Arms around their shoulders.*) We're going to make it. Don't let them get you down. Just keep pitching. You're my rod and my staff and my good right arm. (*Now brisk.*) Look, will you hop to it and lend a hand in the kitchen? We're running out of coffee cups. (LINDA *crosses to do his bidding.*)

MOLLIE. What happened to the dish washer?

CLANCY. He insulted the racial origins of the cook. Of course I couldn't let him stay after that—not Clancy Sussman.

LINDA. Of course not.

MOLLIE. How disgusting.

CLANCY. You're the only ones in my world I can really count on. Even the Danish pastry man let me down today.

MOLLIE. Yes, but he was here last week when you weren't. He was stuck with all that stuff.

LINDA. That's not very sound business, Clancy.

CLANCY. Well let's not worry about him. Now hurry, will you? Clear those tables first.

(CLANCY *goes off with guitars, as* MOLLIE *and* LINDA
start to clear tables.)

LINDA. (*Thoughtfully.*) The most extraordinary thing.
Every dish washer Clancy ever hires is guilty of race
prejudice.

MOLLIE. Linda, were you paid last week?

LINDA. No. Were you?

MOLLIE. (*Crosses up on platform.*) No. And I have a
feeling the dish washer wasn't either. You know, very
often that sort of thing can lead to race prejudice.

(*The* GIRLS *disappear into kitchen with dishes. In a
moment,* ALEX *comes in and peers around blindly in
the gloom.* ALEX *has grown up considerably since we
first met him both in appearance and manner.*
CLANCY *spots him and approaches.*)

ALEX. Hi, Clancy— (*Even* CLANCY *can't see too well.*)

CLANCY. Oh, Alex Loomis. Hi. You all alone?

ALEX. Yes, of course. What the hell have you done to
the lighting in here?

CLANCY. (*Ushering him to a table.*) Well, the New
England Gas and Light Company and I are having a
slight disagreement. I can read a meter, too. I didn't take
all that science for nothing. (*Holds chair for* ALEX.)
They've been making patsies out of the consumers for
years. So I just put my foot down.

ALEX. And they put the lights out. (*Looks around.*)
Where are the Bobbsey twins?

CLANCY. (*With aplomb.*) They're back in their dressing room—resting. (*Picks up menu.*) You just missed
them. (*Waves to an imaginary customer who is leaving.*)
Good night, Joe. Come again. (*Back to* ALEX.) Want to
see a menu? (*He hands* ALEX *a menu, then lights a small
pencil flashlight and holds it so that* ALEX *can read.*)
The Danish pastry is gone, we're out of hamburgers, and
coffee is twenty cents tonight.

ALEX. Mine genial host, I really didn't drop in for

coffee. I'm doing free lance journalism, and I think there's a story in this place—you, the girls, how to become independently wealthy while still an undergraduate.

CLANCY. Independently wealthy! Ha ha— All right. I'll give you a story. (*Yells toward kitchen.*) Hey, kids! Two large coffees and a pizza!

MOLLIE. (*Off Stage Left.*) Coming up!

CLANCY. (*Sits.*) Alex, when I opened this place, my idea was to have the equivalent of the country store—a Paris bistro in the middle of Boston—a stimulus to the free and easy exchange of ideas. Put that down on a piece of paper and take it to the bank and see what kind of credit you get! Their grubby little minds are interested only in the dollar. *People* don't matter. Let me tell you something, Alex, certain monied interests are out to get me!

ALEX. (*He is looking at* CLANCY, *fascinated.*) Clancy, you're crazy.

MOLLIE. (*She comes in, carrying a tray with two coffee cups and an order of pizza. She and* ALEX *exchange impersonal greetings, as she hands out the food, quite inefficiently.*) That's the last of the pizza.

CLANCY. (*Gets up, outraged. The whole world is against him.*) The pizza man didn't show either?

MOLLIE. Nope.

CLANCY. (*To* ALEX.) You see what I mean?

ALEX. (*Looks at pizza doubtfully.*) Is that last night's?

MOLLIE. (*Matter-of-factly.*) We weren't open last night. (ALEX *pushes the pizza away slowly with his hand.*)

CLANCY. What are you pushing it away for?

ALEX. Who pushed it? It moved by itself. (MOLLIE *laughs.*)

CLANCY. Thanks, baby. Loomis here wants to interview you later, for the papers. (*He pats her on the fanny. She slaps his hand away, and goes.*) You used to date Mollie, didn't you? What happened?

ALEX. When I used to date Mollie, I was as obnoxious as you are now—and she told me so.

CLANCY. Ha, Ha. (FRANK, *looking different from his California self in overcoat and hat, comes in and stumbles in the darkness.*) Excuse me. There's a customer. (FRANK *bumps into a table.* CLANCY *reaches him in time to steady him.*)

FRANK. (*Uncertainly.*) Are you—er—open?

CLANCY. (*Grandly.*) Do you have a reservation?

FRANK. I tried to call, but they told me the phone was disconnected.

CLANCY. (*To* ALEX.) Hear that, Alex? They'll stop at nothing.

FRANK. I beg your pardon.

CLANCY. (*Smoothly.*) It just so happens that I can seat you. Here. (CLANCY *seats* FRANK *at a table next to* ALEX's, *hands him the menu and holds the flashlight.*)

FRANK. Thank you.

CLANCY. (*Laconically.*) No Danish pastry, no hamburgers.

ALEX. (*Sotto voce.*) And no pizza.

CLANCY. Just coffee.

FRANK. (*Attempting humor.*) In that case I won't need my Diners' Club card.

CLANCY. We don't honor Diners' Club cards.

FRANK. You don't?

CLANCY. They're inflationary. What'll you have?

FRANK. I put myself in your hands. Whatever you decide.

(CLANCY, *starts off, has an idea. He stops at* ALEX's *table and goes into a whispered conference about the pizza.* ALEX *shrugs.* CLANCY *picks up the pizza and brings it to Frank.*)

CLANCY. Aaah, we're in luck. My friend here was just about to start on his third order, when he realized he'd over-estimated his appetite. And so—you might as well pay for it.

FRANK. Oh, good. (*To* ALEX.) Thank you. I'm just off a plane from California and I'm really starved.

ALEX. (*Not at all sure.*) It's quite all right.

(CLANCY *shambles off.* FRANK *turns his attention to the pizza. First he picks up his fork and works away, realizes he is getting nowhere. Then he takes the knife and attacks it, sawing away ineffectually. Studies the problem a moment. He looks around to be sure nobody is watching, then picks up the pizza and tries to tear it. This gets him nowhere. Finally he gives up, wipes his hands on napkin. He looks at* ALEX.)

FRANK. I beg your pardon. Did I hear correctly? Did you really eat two of these?

ALEX. (*Shakes his head.*) According to The Harvard Crimson, Duncan Hines ate his last meal here.

FRANK. Oh. (*Settles back.*) In that case, I'll just wait for the floor show.

ALEX. The what?

FRANK. The floor show. There's a floor show, isn't there?

ALEX. Oh! Oh, the two girls.

FRANK. Yes, I'll just wait and see them.

ALEX. (*Doubtfully.*) Oh.

FRANK. (*Takes a moment.*) Are they that bad?

ALEX. Well, frankly—

FRANK. (*Cutting him off.*) Please, no! I haven't got the strength for a frank opinion. Before you go any further, I ought to tell you one of them is my daughter. (*Turns back.*)

ALEX. You're Mr. Michaelson.

FRANK. How did you know?

ALEX. Well I've taken Mollie out and I know she's from California—and the other one isn't. (*Hitching his chair closer.*) I'm Alex Loomis. (*They shake hands.*)

FRANK. How do you do?

LINDA. (*She comes out of the kitchen and sets a coffee cup in front of* FRANK. *A statement.*) You don't want cream and sugar, do you.

FRANK. (*Intimidated.*) No. I guess I don't.

(LINDA *starts off Left.*)

ALEX. (*Rises.*) Linda, where's Mollie?
LINDA. She's in the kitchen washing the dishes.

(*She goes.* FRANK *stares after her, then turns to look at* ALEX.)

ALEX. (*Sits.*) Don't look so pained, Mr. Michaelson. At Bennington dishwashing is a three-credit course.
FRANK. (*He sighs and has some coffee. Looks surprised.*) This coffee's all right!
ALEX. It's instant. What can they do to it? Mr. Michaelson, I hope I didn't give you the wrong impression about the girls. They're not too bad. They're just going through a stage, but it's nothing you have to go into hiding about. They'll get over it. (*Turns back.*)
FRANK. Say that again! The first part.
ALEX. I said they're just going through a stage.
FRANK. That's exactly what I've been saying! All the way across on the plane I kept saying "That's all it is—a stage." It's very interesting that that's been your observation too.
ALEX. It's easy for me to see it now. I've been through it. When I was a sophomore, I went home for Christmas and I gave my father—a nervous breakdown.
FRANK. How is your father now?
ALEX. He was making very good progress, but my kid brother started Princeton this year, and—
FRANK. (*Nods his understanding.*) Tell me honestly, don't you think these kids are a little nuttier than they have to be?
ALEX. No. Not really. You see, your generation expects this generation to save the world. You keep watching us. Everybody expects us to be scientists or specialists, which we're perfectly willing to be. But after seven or eight years of all that going to school, what's the first thing

you do with us? You clap us in the army. All that training to become a private first class!

FRANK. Then according to you, we ought to be grateful you're not twice as nutty as you are?

ALEX. I think so.

MOLLIE. (*She comes scuttling out of the kitchen, wearing a large apron over her dress. She slides into a seat beside ALEX.*) Alex, do you mind if I sit with you and pretend I'm a date?

ALEX. What's Clancy up to now? Got you mingling with the customers?

MOLLIE. No, no. There's a city inspector out in the kitchen giving Clancy a terrible time. Linda's hiding in the broom closet. You see, neither one of us is a licensed food handler!

FRANK. Thank God!

MOLLIE. I beg your pardon?

FRANK. I said thank God you're not a licensed food handler!

MOLLIE. (*Gets up.*) Daddy! What are you doing here?

FRANK. (*Stands up, too.*) It's father-daughter weekend, so I know what I'm doing here. But the question nobody'll ever be able to answer is—what the hell are *you* doing here?

(*As he gestures her out of the coffee shop, LIGHTS ARE OUT. LIGHTS COME UP on bare stage [exterior campus]. It is early morning, and the CHAPEL BELLS are heard ringing. After a moment, FRANK comes into scene and looks around, apparently lost. He stops an imaginary girl who is walking past.*)

FRANK. I beg your pardon, but I'm going to classes with my daughter this morning, and she told me to meet her outside of Spencer Hall. I wonder if you could— (*Listens.*) Oh, I'm standing right in front of it? Thank you very much.

(The girl evidently goes on her way. Mollie in a loose coat thrown over her dress, books in her arms, enters.)

Mollie. Hi, Daddy.
Frank. Morning, dear. We're not late, are we?
Mollie. No. We have a few minutes yet. I'm so glad you're here.
Frank. Where did you think I'd be?
Mollie. After last night—maybe on the plane back to California.
Frank. No. I'm anxious to see what the academic side of life in the east is like.
Mollie. *(Her head on his shoulder.)* Honorable daughter admits coffee house very bad mistake.
Frank. Honorable father agrees.

(The BELLS are heard ringing the hour.)

Mollie. Time for class, Daddy. *(Starts off Right.)*
Frank. What class is it?
Mollie. English 20. Modern Poetry. Mr. Hibbetts.
Frank. The one you wrote us about.
Mollie. Yes.
Frank. The one with the hurt look.
Mollie. You'll just love him.
Frank. Oh, I have very deep feelings about him already. *(They link arms and go off Right.)*

(Stage Center, a CLASSROOM set-up now appears in the form of a double row of attached chairs, a desk with a blackboard behind it. Mr. Hibbetts, a balding bespectacled fellow, is at the desk. He removes his glasses and polishes them, blinking his eyes in the glare: the hurt look. Then he turns and writes on the blackboard the name—Liam McTeague. Through this, Mollie and Frank have come in. There are apparently other fathers and daughters attending the class, but they are not seen. Mollie

tries to snag two seats in the back row, but somebody apparently gets there first. She captures two seats in the middle for herself and FRANK, *and gestures someone else to the seat in front of them. She and* FRANK *settle down.* FRANK *takes a good look at* HIBBETTS *and then looks doubtfully at* MOLLIE, *who looks straight ahead.* HIBBETTS *"ers" constantly when he speaks. It's not that the fathers make him nervous; he does it all the time.)*

HIBBETTS. (*A toothy smile.*) On behalf of the English Department—er—I should like to extend a welcome to—er—those of you who have come to observe—er—and we hope you will not only observe—er—but also participate. If there are any questions which you would like to ask, please feel free to—er—throw them at me and I'll do my best to—er—field them. (HIBBETTS *feels that this figure of speech has made him one of the boys and he laughs.* FRANK *manages to bare his teeth in response. Exchanges an uncomfortable look with* MOLLIE.) Today I thought we might pursue our study of the—er—poetry of Liam McTeague. As I said the last time we met—er—unfortunately McTeague, one of the—finest of the moderns, seems to be known—by the general public more for his—er—drinking habits than for his—er—exquisite poetry. Although—er—in fairness, McTeague has done more than his—er—share in—*projecting* this image. As for example when asked by the BBC to read the following poem—er—on the air—he arrived somewhat under the—er—influence of the—er—grape and—er—completely rewrote it—and was cut off in the middle. (*This ends on a note of surprise.* FRANK *exchanges another look with* MOLLIE.) Well, enough of that. Here is, I suppose, what one might call the—er—watered-down version of that—er—poem. (*He laughs again, feeling he has made a joke.* FRANK *rests his chin on the palm of his hand and does his best to look intelligent and interested.*) It is called "Life, Death, and a Small Installment Due." (*He opens book and reads:*)

"Kickingly, pantingly squallingly
Outwardly thrusting
In pain and shock and disbelief
Hopingly, graspingly, aspiringly
Trustfully demanding
Through all pre-recorded
Synchronized and sealed
Impermanently permanent
Yet scrimpingly, sparingly, clingingly
Scheming and striving
For millions and monuments
Marbles and millstones
Negating the ultimate
All interest canceled
Repossessed"

Liverpool, 1956.

FRANK. (*His chin slips out of the palm of his hand. Whispers to* MOLLIE.) Well—that last part's clear.
MOLLIE. Sh!

(MR. HIBBETTS' *birdlike glance picks him up.*)

HIBBETTS. Did you want to comment, Mr.—er— This *is* your father, isn't it, Mollie?
MOLLIE. (*Nervously.*) Yes, Mr. Hibbetts.
HIBBETTS. Did you want to comment, Mr. Michaelson?
FRANK. Er—no—er—not particularly.
HIBBETTS. Well, did the poem have any impact?
FRANK. Oh, yes, yes. Definitely.
HIBBETTS. I see. (*To the other non-existent class members.*) Any other comments? (*Apparently there are none. He falls back on* FRANK *to keep the discussion alive.*) Mr.—er—Michaelson, I can't help feeling that you—er— *did* have—er—something to say, and I wish you wouldn't feel—er—inhibited. Just feel—er—free to speak. For example, what—er—image did the poem suggest to you, if—er—any?

FRANK. (*Leans forward.*) Well, it suggested the image of a fellow who was having quite a bit of trouble with the Household Finance Corporation. (MOLLIE *is clasping her hands together, and has her face turned away.* FRANK *looks hopefully at Hibbetts.*) Am I on the right track?

HIBBETTS. (*Carefully.*) I don't think McTeague has ever—er—been evaluated in such—er—practical, everyday terms . . .

FRANK. Well, I'm not really a very good judge of this sort of thing. I think I agree with—I think it was Bernard Shaw—who said: "Every man should be a poet at twenty-one, and any man who's still a poet at thirty is a first-class fool." (MOLLIE, *in pain, sinks down in seat and covers her face with her hand.*)

HIBBETTS. (*Polishing his glasses.*) As I recall, Shaw said that about Socialists.

FRANK. Oh, no. Shaw was a Socialist to the end. He said that about poets. How old is this McTeague?

HIBBETTS. I'm not quite sure. I'll have to look that up. (*Consults his book.*)

MOLLIE. (*Hissing in* FRANK'S *ear.*) Daddy, Daddy, Mr. Hibbetts writes poetry!

FRANK. How old is he?

MOLLIE. Old enough to flunk me.

FRANK. (*Whispering.*) Gee, I'm sorry, honey. Why didn't you tell me?

MOLLIE. Who thought you'd get involved in a—?

(FRANK *realizes that* MOLLIE *is upset. He thinks a moment, then raises his hand as if he were in the first grade.* MR. HIBBETTS *doesn't see this.* FRANK *waves his hand in the air. Still no effect on* HIBBETTS.)

FRANK. Oh, Mr. Hibbetts—

HIBBETTS. Yes, Mr. Michaelson?

FRANK. (*Rises.*) Don't bother looking that up. As I recall, you're quite right. Shaw *did* say that about Socialists, not poets.

HIBBETTS. (*Relieved.*) Oh, thank you.

FRANK. (*A whisper to* MOLLIE; *two heads together.*) I think I fixed that, don't you?

MOLLIE. Yes, Daddy. (*Realizes* HIBBETTS *is looking at them.*) Shhhh.

HIBBETTS. Mollie, if you—er—have any comments to make—er—I wish you wouldn't keep them in the—er—bosom of the family but would—er—let us all share them.

MOLLIE. Well, I didn't really—

HIBBETTS. Oh? McTeague has no impact on you whatever?

MOLLIE. (*Something in Hibbetts' tone irritates her.*) Well, frankly, Mr. Hibbetts, I find McTeague empty.

HIBBETTS. Well—er—perhaps that's—er—what he wants you to feel.

MOLLIE. But I just don't feel *anything.* In every one of his poems, at least the ones I've read, he seems to find all of existence so utterly futile, as if life were just—an intermission between—two shocking events, birth and death. Which, I suppose, is why he's always drinking or rotting, or throwing his life away, or whatever. He seems completely preoccupied with the obvious fact that from the day we're born we're all rushing toward death. Life is full of so many beautiful things which he seems to ignore entirely. (*A pause for breath.*) In other words, I'm in complete agreement with the previous speaker!

(FRANK *beams at her. Together he and* MOLLIE *get up and come Downstage Right as CLASSROOM moves off. They are now EXTERIOR CAMPUS.*)

FRANK. Gee, Mollie, I thought you were just great.

MOLLIE. Thanks, Daddy. (*Thoughtfully.*) You know, Mr. Hibbetts looked different today—I'm not even sure he's a good teacher.

FRANK. He's a good teacher. He's fine. (*Looks around, delighted with his view of the campus. With enthusiasm.*) Where do we go now?

MOLLIE. Medieval History.

FRANK. You'll be glad to hear I don't know a damn thing about Medieval History. (*Thoughtfully.*) Of course I don't know anything about modern poetry either, still— (*They stroll across Stage together.*)

MOLLIE. After Medieval History, there's an art exhibition with the usual lecturer. Then there's a lunch with the Dean of Women—then an archery contest on the lawn. After that, there's the father-daughter ping-pong tournament. (*Stops, Stage Left.*) Linda Lehman's father defaulted, so I rushed down and got their place for us.

FRANK. Well, come on. Let's get going.

MOLLIE. How do you feel?

FRANK. Just great.

MOLLIE. You know sometimes I think the wrong Michaelson is going to college. (*She takes his arm and they go off Stage Left.*)

(*As the DORMITORY comes on, lit for evening, a chorus of* GIRLS' VOICES *is heard singing the Hawthorne Alma Mater, to the tune of "O, Tannenbaum."*)

GIRLS'S VOICES. (*Singing.*)
    "O Hawthorne, O Hawthorne,
    Beside the shining waters.
    O Hawthorne, O Hawthorne,
    We're proud to be your daughters.

    We pledge our faith, our honor true,
    With grateful hearts we sing to you.

    O Hawthorne, O Hawthorne,
    We're proud to be your daughters."

(*In the course of the song,* MOLLIE *comes into the room, followed by* FRANK, *who staggers slightly.*)

MOLLIE. (*As she comes in.*) It's 5:30, Daddy. You haven't got time to go back to the hotel. I told you.

FRANK. Which bed is yours?

MOLLIE. This one, right here. (*He collapses onto it, unaware that he is lying on a stuffed animal.*) Now, Daddy, you can't pass out on me.

FRANK. (*Not convinced.*) Can't I?

MOLLIE. Well, there's still the banquet and two one-act plays by Ionesco—

FRANK. (*Sits up; feebly.*) Two?

MOLLIE. Two. And then the dance.

FRANK. Where's that held? In the infirmary? Mollie, get me a drink, will you?

MOLLIE. Sure, Daddy. Be right back. And remember— don't pass out! (*She goes, Stage Left. He shows every intention of doing just that. SARAH comes into the room and looks at him.*)

SARAH. Oh, it's Mr. Michaelson. I'm Sarah Walker.

FRANK. (*Sadly, trying to rise.*) I wish you hadn't done that. Now I have to get up.

SARAH. (*Sits on other bed.*) No. Please don't. I understand.

MOLLIE. (*She dashes back in with a glass of water.*) Here, Daddy. (*Then crosses to desk.*) Hi, Sarah.

FRANK. (*Sits up and takes glass.*) Thank you, dear.

SARAH. I hear you got to the finals in the ping-pong tournament.

FRANK. Yes, and we'd have won, if we hadn't got that bad call. (*Has a swallow, sputters with indignation.*) Water! Don't they *teach* you anything at this college?

MOLLIE. Daddy, you can get kicked out of school for— (*Changing.*) Sarah, where's your mouth wash?

SARAH. On the book shelf— (MOLLIE *crosses to door.*) behind Dewey's "Moral Principles of Education."

MOLLIE. I'll only be a minute. (*She rushes out. FRANK lies back and closes his eyes.*)

FRANK. Drink or no drink, I don't think I'm going to be able to make it. My back is killing me.

SARAH. (*Rises, crosses to bed.*) Excuse me, Mr. Michaelson. (*She reaches under the small of his back, pulls out the stuffed animal and hands it to him.*)

FRANK. Oh, hello, Pluto. I gave him to Mollie on her fourth birthday. He's the only one of us who hasn't changed.

MOLLIE. (*She is back with a large bottle labeled "Mouth Wash." Gives* FRANK *bottle.*) Here you are, Daddy.

· FRANK. (*He pours a hefty slug into his glass. She takes bottle, crosses to bed, sits.* FRANK *sniffs the aroma appreciatively.*) Aaaaah.. Well, I'm being kicked out tomorrow anyway so—cheers! (*He downs the drink.*)

(ADELE *sticks her head in the doorway.*)

ADELE. Mollie— (*Gestures to indicate she'd like* MOLLIE *to come out.*)

MOLLIE. Excuse me a minute, Daddy. (*She puts bottle on floor.* ADELE *and* MOLLIE *go.*)

FRANK. Mollie said your father didn't come this weekend.

SARAH. Not one of them. (*Leans forward.*) I thought I wouldn't mind—but I do.

FRANK. What are you planning to do when you—?

SARAH. Graduate? (*He nods.*) Oh, take my Master's, then my Ph.D. Then I'll teach. I'm not going out in the real world. Everybody out there is miserable. I'm staying right here. Is that a very young idea?

FRANK. I understand what you mean. Everybody drinks too much or eats too much or thinks about himself too much. (*Takes sip.*)

SARAH. Or sleeps around too much.

FRANK. Oh, don't go by John O'Hara novels. That's mostly wishful thinking— (*Drinks.*) among the people I know, anyway. (FRANK *gropes for bottle.* SARAH *gets it and pours him another.*) Thank you. You really want to teach?

SARAH. Oh, yes. I know it's a surprise to everybody, but I get very good grades. (MOLLIE *comes back into room, looking disturbed,* SARAH *senses it, and turns to go.*) Well, thank you, Mr. Michaelson.

FRANK. What for?

SARAH. For being a listener. (*Starts out.*) Well, have a ball. I hear the kitchen is going all out to serve what they consider a Roman banquet — grape juice and fried chicken. (*She is gone.*)

MOLLIE. You can freshen up in the bathroom. (*Indicates the direction.*) I'm going to wear the blue you gave me for Christmas.

FRANK. Good. I like that dress. (FRANK *disappears in direction of bathroom, Left.* MOLLIE *kicks off her shoes, and changes to the blue dress, in course of scene. From Offstage.*) You know, Mollie, frankly last night I had some doubts about this. Took me quite a while to fall asleep. That Clancy Sussman is pretty hard to digest. Anyway, today was marvelous. Seeing this place, and going to class with you, and being around young people. Even meeting Liam McTeague for the first time. (*Intoning.*) Inwardly, Outwardly, Kickingly, Pantingly— (*Then singing.*) *Inwardly, Outwardly, Kickingly, Pantingly*— It made me feel it was all good. That it wasn't a mistake. I can't wait to get home and tell your mother what a wonderful—

MOLLIE. (*Cutting him off, almost in tears.*) Oh, Daddy!

FRANK. (*He re-enters.*) Yes, Mollie?

MOLLIE. Nothing, Daddy.

FRANK. Nothing?

MOLLIE. Can you zip me up?

FRANK. (*Carrying his coat and knotting his tie.*) Sure. Say, I like that dress. I have good taste in women's clothes. I don't know why, but I have. (*Zips her up and fastens hook.*)

MOLLIE. (*Turns to* FRANK.) Daddy—

FRANK. Yes, Mollie?

MOLLIE. You remember I wrote you about that fellowship to go abroad this summer?

FRANK. With the State Department. Of course.

MOLLIE. That's what Adele wanted to see me about. She just saw the list in her sister's office. And my name wasn't on it.

FRANK. (*Clears his throat.*) I'm sorry.

MOLLIE. So am I.

FRANK. Only because you wanted it. It really isn't important.

MOLLIE. Oh, yes it is. It's very important.

FRANK. (*Thinks a moment.*) It's just a summer in Europe doing some sort of paper work which may or may not be socially significant. So what? (*Turns her to face him.*) If you want to go to Europe this summer—

MOLLIE. (*Crosses above* FRANK *to bed Left.*) It isn't that. .

FRANK. (*Follows* MOLLIE *up.*) But I can send you. And I think you'd learn a lot more going around on a bicycle.

MOLLIE. That has nothing to do with it. (*Crosses Right; shakes her head.*) I failed, don't you see? (*Turns.*) The first time in my life I wanted something and I didn't get it. And you can't give it to me—you can't. (*Being relentless with herself.*) I thought I was so sharp—I'd walk in and they'd fall all over themselves to get me. (*Sits on bed Center.*) I just got a picture of what I must have looked like. Even you wouldn't have given me the job.

FRANK. (*Sits next to* MOLLIE.) Oh, honey—

MOLLIE. Daddy, I'm so far away from what you want. What you must think of me—

FRANK. (*Takes her chin in his hand.*) What I think of you? Mollie, let's get one thing straight. If they sent me the news that you had burned down the college and murdered the Dean—I would forgive you. It's what you think of yourself that matters.

MOLLIE. (*Head on* FRANK's *shoulder.*) I'm so ashamed.

FRANK. If you can see that, it's the beginning of getting an education.

MOLLIE. Are you shrinking my head?

FRANK. A little. Come on now. (*Rises.*) We're going to a dance tonight, and we'll be the coolest couple on the floor. Here— (*Offers a handkerchief.*) Dry your eyes.

(MOLLIE *manages a smile, rises, goes to mirror and looks at herself.* FRANK *gets her evening purse from desk.*)

MOLLIE. God, I look awful.

FRANK. (*Looking over her shoulder at mirror.*) Hideous, but you're my date and I'm stuck with you. I may not look like much myself but I'll bet I'm the only father at Hawthorne College who's studied the rhumba for two solid years.

(*He offers his arm, and they exit grandly. DORMITORY OFF. CAMPUS FENCE appears, lit for day.* ALEX *is leaning against it, pretending to be reading. He looks off Stage Left, apparently waiting for someone. Then he looks Stage Right, and sees someone coming. He goes to other side of fence, turns his back and reads, to avoid being seen. In a moment,* SARAH *comes on Stage Right, accompanied by* 1ST FRESH-MAN.)

1ST FRESHMAN. What was that author's name again?

SARAH. Kafka.

1ST FRESHMAN. (*Pretending great interest.*) Mmmhmm.

SARAH. He wrote "Metamorphosis." It's really a very strange story.

1ST FRESHMAN. Oh, sure—"Metamorphosis."

SARAH. It's all about this man who wakes up one morn-ing and finds out he's a cockroach.

1ST FRESHMAN. Yeh.

SARAH. And his family locks him in his room— What do you suppose Kafka means by that? (*They walk across the stage together.*)

1ST FRESHMAN. Oh, I read that story. As I analyze it, aside from the fact that it's mortifying to have a cock-roach in the family, this man had a sense of guilt because he was trying to displace his own father. (*They stop.*)

SARAH. Then he really did it to himself?

1ST FRESHMAN. Conceivably. (*Pause.*) By the way, what are you doing tonight?

SARAH. Why?

1ST FRESHMAN. Well, I thought we could pursue this discussion further and see where it gets us.

(*They are off, Stage Left. ALEX looks after them, evidently sees someone coming. He moves to other side of fence and again pretends to be engrossed in his book. MOLLIE comes on slowly from Left. She is in a sweater and skirt, and carries some books and a small sheaf of green leaves. She walks right past ALEX without seeing him. This brings him to his feet.*)

ALEX. Hello.

MOLLIE. (*Bemused.*) Oh, hello, Alex.

ALEX. (*Looks at her curiously.*) Something the matter?

MOLLIE. No. I'm just a million miles away. We don't have any spring in California, you see. Aren't they lovely?

ALEX. What? (*She indicates the leaves.*) The leaves? Oh, yes, yes, they're beautiful.

MOLLIE. The woods are full of wild flowers, but it seemed a shame to pick them.

ALEX. (*After a blank look at her; sits on rail.*) Can we talk? Or are you in a hurry?

MOLLIE. (*Leans on rail, Right.*) Oh, no. I'm never in a hurry. People hurry too much—through life. (*Quoting.*) "The complexities of civilization stand in the way of significant living."

ALEX. That rings a bell. It's a quote.

MOLLIE. Is there *anything* you don't know?

ALEX. Oh, so much— There's so little I know outside of books—it's driving me nuts.

MOLLIE. Everybody has his problems.

ALEX. (*Sits on rail.*) And you're solving yours by communing with nature. (*Snaps his fingers.*) I've got it! Thoreau! (*Looks at her.*) Are you going through that bit now?

MOLLIE. What bit?

ALEX. The Thoreau bit. You know, living the simple life, eating nuts and berries, playing with the pickerel in the pond—

MOLLIE. (*Annoyed.*) The pickerel in the pond! Honestly, you leap to the most ridiculous conclusions. (*Moves to* ALEX; *he backs away a few steps.*) Just because I happened to quote Thoreau! Life isn't just one thing or another. It's a combination of things.

ALEX. (*Sorry he started this.*) All right.

MOLLIE. You intellectualize so much. You put labels on everything.

ALEX. All right, Mollie, all right.

MOLLIE. (*She walks away from him, stops, her back to him. Stiffly.*) What did you want to see me about?

ALEX. (*Raises his hands helplessly.*) I have the feeling if I tell you now, you'll cheer, maybe.

MOLLIE. (*Turns.*) I might. What is it?

ALEX. I came to say good-bye.

MOLLIE. Oh.

ALEX. I've finished my Master's and I'm not coming back.

MOLLIE. Now, why did you think I'd want to cheer because you came to say good-bye? That's a terrible thing to say.

ALEX. Mollie, that's the story of our relationship. I always say the wrong thing to you.

MOLLIE. Are your prospects good ones?

ALEX. Yes. All of them. Very.

MOLLIE. That's very nice for you.

ALEX. I don't know why I'm hostile. I don't really mean to be. It's just my manner. Last time I saw you we got into a violent argument about Italian movies. I couldn't care less about Italian movies!

MOLLIE. Well, you don't really need that manner any more, Alex. It's all right for someone like me, who's all waste motion, just floundering about—

ALEX. (*Gently.*) Mollie—

MOLLIE. Please! I just can't stand sympathy. (*A pause.*) I'm sure I'll hear about you—or read about you.

ALEX. (*He takes her hand.*) Mollie, let's have dinner tonight.

MOLLIE. I can't. I take my last final tomorrow, and I've got to cram all night. Contemporary History. I'm having an awful time with contemporary history.

ALEX. Tomorrow night, then.

MOLLIE. I'm taking the plane home tomorrow afternoon. (*Silence for a moment; drop hands.*) Good-bye, Alex. Thank you.

ALEX. (*Moves Left.*) Good-bye, Mollie. (*Starts off, stops.*) Goddammit, good-bye! (*He goes off Left.*)

(MOLLIE *is alone. She starts off Right, changes her mind, stops and looks after* ALEX. *She hesitates, appears about to call after him, then shakes her head. She sighs `and goes off. LIGHTS GO OUT SLOWLY. There is the sound of AIRPLANE NOISES. Stage Left, a BARBECUE has appeared, its back to audience.* ANNE, *in slacks and shirt, is fanning the fire. Center Stage, a garden table and chairs and a chaise-longue´ are seen.* LIZ *comes out of house from Right, looking somewhat grown up, with her hair pulled back off her forehead with a band, and sunglasses on. She wears tight pants and a flapping shirt.*)

LIZ. How's the fire doing, Mom?

ANNE. Fine. (*Looks around in the still-bright light.*) Oh, I hate the summers in California. I wonder if it's raining any place. I'd like to go there.

LIZ. (*Sits and takes off glasses.*) Not me. I'm having the most marvelous summer.

ANNE. Are you dear? I'm glad. (FRANK *comes out; crosses to lounge, sits and opens newspaper.*) What was on the news?

FRANK. "Good night, Chet." "Good night, David." (*Reads paper.*) Those two are such a comfort to each other. Where's her Royal Highness?

ANNE. Incommunicado.

Liz. She's in her room. She's got a sign on her door: "Ne frappez pas à cette porte."

Anne. Resting?

Liz. (*Shakes her head.*) I thought I heard her working on that crazy stenotype machine she's so goofy about.

Frank. I'd like to frappez on her—

Anne. Frank!

Liz. (*Importantly.*) Mom, Daddy, there's something I want to talk to you about. (*Reacting to her own tone.*) Gosh! Sounds like I'm having a baby!

Frank. Are you?

Liz. (*Gets up.*) No, of course not.

Frank. Well, don't scare us like that, will you?

Liz. Don't worry about that. I'm a great believer in planned parenthood. What I want to talk to you about is . . .

(*The PHONE has started to ring through that.*)

Anne. That's the phone.

Frank. Would you get it, honey?

Liz. Oh, sure, sure. Don't go 'way. (*She goes into house.*)

Frank. (*Gets up and crosses to* Anne.) Look, I don't want anybody to get the wrong impression. (*Belligerently.*) It's perfectly all right with me if Mollie quits college. There's nothing wrong with her becoming a court stenographer. It's a perfectly good job.

Anne. And it pays very well.

Frank. Also, it's high time somebody else brought some money into this house.

(Liz *comes back.*)

Anne. Who was that on the phone?

Liz. A boy, for Mollie.

Anne. Did you frappez on her porte?

Liz. No. I yellayed up the stairs.

Frank. (*Takes a good look at her.*) What are you

dressed up as? You know, if I had wanted a son, I'd have had one!

Liz. Daddy, I've been wearing this all summer.

Frank. Then it's about time you changed.

Liz. Well, I have something to say first.

Frank. I'm sure you have. (*Brusquely.*) I left two drinks on the bar. Would you bring them out here?

Liz. Oh, sure. (*Going.*) I wish Lincoln had freed the children, too! (*She is off.*)

Frank. (*Inspecting fire.*) Who built that fire?

Anne. I did. Why?

Frank. Nothing! It's fine. (*Stomps back to chaise.*)

Anne. Frank— (*Sits on chair; he looks at her.*) Let go. You have to let go.

Frank. That's exactly what I'm doing. I'm letting go. I've cut the umbilical cord! (*Accompanies that with a cutting gesture.*)

Anne. *You* have? That's very interesting.

Frank. Well, you know what I mean.

(Mollie's *voice is heard from the upper window.*)

Mollie's Voice. Daddy!

Frank. Yes, Mollie.

Mollie's Voice. Can we handle one extra for dinner? Is there enough steak?

Frank. Yes. Sure.

Mollie's Voice. Good.

Frank. Who?—Who's coming? (*No answer.*) She's gone.

Anne. (*Comfortably.*) Oh, she'll have to introduce him. We'll all be eating at the same table.

(Liz *marches out, carrying two drinks. She hands one to* Anne *and one to* Frank.)

Liz. (*Grimly.*) Here's your drink, Mom. Here's yours, Daddy. Now, will both of you please look at me? (*They look surprised.*) I am your daughter, Elizabeth. I have been trying to say something. It isn't very important, but I'd like to say it!

FRANK. What are you being so dramatic about? If you have something to say, say it.

LIZ. (*A deep breath; to* ANNE.) I have a message for you from Emmett Whitmyer.

FRANK. That little bastard.

LIZ. (*Crosses to* FRANK, *puts her hand on his shoulder.*) Yes. He has an idea you feel that way, and he wonders if he can come over and show you how much he's changed.

FRANK. Who cares whether he's changed or not? Mollie's not interested in him.

LIZ. He's not interested in Mollie.

FRANK. (*Looks up at her, realizes what she means.*) Oh, come on!

LIZ. (*Blazing up.*) What's so wrong with that? Everybody in this house is so busy thinking about Mollie, they don't seem to realize that I'm growing up, too! (*To* ANNE.) It doesn't occur to you that I might have some problems. But if you don't want to discuss them, that's quite all right with me. It doesn't matter in the least! (*A few steps toward house.*) I'm perfectly capable of handling things myself! So you just go on worrying about Mollie. But remember, it won't be long before *I* go away to school, too! I mean, let's get things in proper focus, shall we? (*She stalks off.*)

FRANK. (*He stares after her.*) Maybe the British are right. They don't try to understand children. They just send them away as early as possible.

ANNE. (*Gets up and goes to barbecue.*) Oh, the hell with it. My mother and father never understood me—and I enjoyed it enormously. The hell with them.

MOLLIE. (*She comes in carrying her steno-type machine.*) Hi.

FRANK. (*Without looking up from his paper.*) Hello.

ANNE. Well, aren't you dressed up!

MOLLIE. Do I look all right?

ANNE. Lovely.

FRANK. Who's coming to dinner?

MOLLIE. (*Sits.*) A boy from Harvard.

ANNE. Isn't that nice?

FRANK. (*Reading paper.*) What's so nice about it? I'm not so sure about Harvard as the rest of the country is.

MOLLIE. (*Trying to make him understand.*) But this boy is— (*He doesn't look up from paper; she abandons the attempt.*) Does anybody want to give me some dictation?

FRANK. (*Slaps down newspaper and gets up.*) I'll give you some dictation. "Michaelson versus Michaelson."

ANNE. Oh, the fight of the week. Pardon me. (*She goes into house.*)

FRANK. (*Paces Upstage, as* MOLLIE *works on machine.*) "Case between Frank Michaelson, hereinafter referred to as the plaintiff, and Mollie Michaelson, hereinafter referred to as the defendant." (MOLLIE *throws him a look. He rattles his speech off at breakneck speed.* MOLLIE *tries to follow, then stops.*) "The plaintiff wishes the court to recognize that his case is a simple one. He stipulates that the defendant has been making a damn fool of herself and ought to go back to school and make full use of the brains that God was good enough to give her." Have you got that?

MOLLIE. I got as far as "damn fool."

FRANK. (*Crosses to table.*) Then you got it! Mollie, you have horse-power. You and that machine make as much sense as a—a diesel engine pulling a kiddie car!

MOLLIE. (*Turns front.*) Daddy, don't you realize you have an image of me that doesn't exist? Haven't I proved to you in the last two years that I'm none of the things you want me to be? And college! Your idea of college! That's the biggest riot of all. It's a lot of "will you" or "won't you" or "do you" or "don't you" or "I hope I'm not the first, am I?" Think about that for a while. You talk about it as if it's something. It's nothing. It's just a very small tragedy in a very small life.

(*DOORBELL rings in house.* LIZ's *voice is heard from the house.*)

LIZ'S VOICE. Mollie! The doorbell.
MOLLIE. (*Gets up.*) Would you get it, please.

(FRANK *moves Left slowly.*)

LIZ'S VOICE. I can't. I'm changing.
ANNE'S VOICE. I'll get it, dear.
LIZ'S VOICE. Somebody in this house doesn't approve of the way I dress!
FRANK. (*A gesture of futility.*) I'll go see about the steaks. (*He exits Left.*)

(MOLLIE *moves nervously Left of table, smoothing her dress and her hair. She waits a moment, then starts toward house.* ANNE *appears, showing* ALEX *out to garden.*)

ANNE. Mollie's expecting you.
ALEX. I'm glad.
ANNE. She's right out here. (*Exits.*)
ALEX. Thank you, Mrs. Michaelson. (*He comes out into garden. They look at each other for a moment.*) Hello, Mollie.
MOLLIE. Alex, I'm so glad to see you. What are you doing in Los Angeles?
ALEX. Well, I came here on impulse. I've changed my whole character now. I'm living by impulse rather than by reason.
MOLLIE. Let me know if it works. (*Sits.*)
ALEX. I'm on my way to San Francisco.
MOLLIE. By way of Los Angeles?
ALEX. Yes. (MOLLIE *looks away.*) I came to see you. (MOLLIE *looks at* ALEX; *there is a pause.* ALEX *sits.*) I'm going to Stanford. I've got a teaching fellowship there.
MOLLIE. Congratulations. You came to see me?

ALEX. I wrote you a lot of letters, Mollie. An awful lot of them.

MOLLIE. (*Looks at* ALEX.) You did? (*Looks down.*) I waited for them, but they never came.

ALEX. I tore them all up. I even wrote a speech—but I'm not going to use it. By the way, are you married, or engaged, or anything?

MOLLIE. I'm not married or engaged, and I'm not quite sure what "or anything" means.

ALEX. (*Gets up, has trouble finding words, finally turns to face* MOLLIE.) Mollie, let's be conventional.

MOLLIE. All right. Let's.

ALEX. If I stick around the next couple of weeks before I go to Stanford—will you give me some time?

MOLLIE. Yes—

ALEX. You will?

MOLLIE. Lots of time, Alex.

ALEX. I think I'll read that speech after all. (*Takes it out, reads:*) "Despite many rebuffs, I think about Miss Mollie Michaelson every day, with the following results: A—loss of sleep; B—loss of appetite; C—loss of temper; D—loss of driver's license." (MOLLIE *laughs; he looks up from paper.*) I went through two red lights. I was thinking about Miss Mollie Michaelson. Shall I go on?

MOLLIE. No. I get the idea.

ALEX. Oh, Mollie.

MOLLIE. (*Gets up, a few steps, then:*) I think we're going to have a wonderful two weeks.

ALEX. (*Takes her hands.*) Mollie, I have a great idea. Why don't you transfer to Stanford and finish your education up there? It's really a hell of a school.

MOLLIE. I've finished my education. I've quit college, I'm going to become a court stenographer.

ALEX. You're kidding.

MOLLIE. No. My father is absolutely furious.

ALEX. I should think so. (FRANK *comes out with the steaks on a platter covered with waxed paper. Neither of them sees him.*) It's the most idiotic thing I ever heard of. You might want to go to South Africa and teach, or get

a job with Time Mazazine, or— You need a degree for
that. Of course you can be perfectly well educated without a degree, but why shut those doors on yourself? Who
knows what you'll wind up doing?

MOLLIE. Then you think it's a mistake?

ALEX. I most certainly do. With your capabilities?
With your potential?

MOLLIE. You know, nobody ever quite put it to me in
those terms before.

FRANK. (*He has the look of a man who has been
poleaxed. He stands stunned for a moment.*) Good God!
(*He turns and heaves the steaks at the barbecue, as the
LIGHTS GO OUT.*)

(*AIRPLANE noises are heard. LIGHTS COME UP on
STEEL LINK FENCE leading to plane. The AIR-
LINES ATTENDANT is checking tickets for imaginary
passengers and waving them through the gate. ANNE
and LIZ come on from Left, laden down with LIZ's
possessions. LIZ looks very like Mollie when she first
went off to school—quite grown up, in traveling suit
and hat. LIZ puts a large shapeless bag down, Left,
and crosses Stage in search of her father. ANNE
follows.*)

LIZ. Where's Daddy? If he doesn't get here right away,
I'll be gone.

ANNE. He probably had trouble finding a parking spot.

LIZ. What about that speech about how I have to help
change the world? I have that coming to me.

ANNE. Yes, dear, it's part of the course.

(FRANK *comes rushing in from Left and joins them.*)

FRANK. I thought you were still at the counter.

ANNE. We couldn't wait. They announced the flight.

FRANK. (*Takes LIZ's arm and strolls with her companionably, speaks earnestly.*) Liz, I want you to listen
to me. Now, more than ever, the world is facing the

challenge of new ideas. Radcliffe, in its own way, is in a class with great schools like—

LIZ. (*She evidently sees somebody going past; leaves her father.*) Hi, Barbara—Daddy, Mom, this is Mr. and Mrs. Treback. Barbara's going to Hawthorne. (*There is an exchange of greetings.*) Have you got your seat yet? (LIZ *and* BARBARA *move off to Left for a private conversation.*)

FRANK. Our other daughter went there for two years. She just switched to Stanford. . . . Oh, no. She loved Hawthorne. But you see, her fiance is a professor at Stanford.

ANNE. A professor!

FRANK. (*Ignores that.*) And—well— (MOLLIE *and* ALEX *come in from Right, arm-in-arm, and all wrapped up in each other. They are dressed for travel.*) There they are. See what I mean? (ANNE *excuses herself and joins* MOLLIE *and* ALEX. FRANK *speaks in a confidential tone.*) You know, of the two, Liz being more balanced, might just possibly be— (*Taps the side of his head sagely.*)

LIZ. You better get in line.

FRANK. (*Waving good-bye.*) Well, see you at Christmas— (*Calling after them.*) Oh, by the way, don't miss father-daughter week-end at Hawthorne— A little expensive, but you'll have a ball! (LIZ *is also waving good-bye. He turns her around to face him. She listens obediently.* ANNE *rejoins them.*) Now, Liz, I want you to take full advantage of the Harvard faculty—

(EMMETT *comes into scene looking very grown up, he thinks, and a little too Ivy League—raincoat slung over one shoulder, small suitcase in hand.*)

ANNE. Oh, Emmett.

LIZ. Hi, Emmett.

EMMETT. Hello, Mrs. Michaelson. Good evening, sir— Well, it certainly has been a long time.

FRANK. Not long enough for—

ANNE. (*Cutting in.*) Are you on this flight, too?

EMMETT. Yes. Don't worry about Elizabeth, sir. I'll keep an eye on her for you.

FRANK. Thank you. (LIZ *and* EMMETT *drift off Left for a whispered consultation.*) Just what I need to guarantee a good night's sleep.

LIZ. (*She rejoins them, leaving* EMMETT.) Daddy, you don't have to have any fears about Emmett. I've got him completely under control.

ANNE. They're loading, dear.

LIZ. I'm going! Good-bye, everybody!

(*She kisses her* MOTHER *and* FATHER, *and her possessions are piled into her arms in a flurry of ad libs. She kisses* MOLLIE, *then offers her hand to* ALEX, *who gives her a fraternal kiss on the cheek. She throws a look of blissful envy at* MOLLIE, *then goes through gate. They wave and call after her a final salvo of* "good-bye" *and* "don't forget to write," *etc. As* LIZ *passes* EMMETT *at Left end of fence, she stops and points imperiously to her large bag.* EMMETT *picks it up and swings it over the fence to her. All watch as she goes off.* EMMETT *now picks up his own small bag, and proceeds in a very dignified, somewhat martial manner to the ticket taker. He hands over his ticket, turns to exchange a bland smile with* MOLLIE, *and he goes.* FRANK *and* ANNE *now turn to* MOLLIE *and* ALEX.)

FRANK. What gate is your plane?

ALEX. It hasn't been announced. We have an hour yet.

MOLLIE. Look, there's really no reason for you two to hang around the airport all that time.

(ANNE *throws a look at* FRANK, *to see what effect that had on him.*)

FRANK. No . . . I . . . I guess not. Well, good-bye. (*Shakes* ALEX'S *hand.*)

MOLLIE. Good-bye, Mom. Good-bye, Daddy. (*There is*

another exchange of kisses, a little stiff and formal, after which they break apart, and MOLLIE *and* ALEX *start off Right.* FRANK *and* ANNE *stand and watch them go. They are almost off, when* MOLLIE *stops and looks back at her parents.*) Daddy! Mom! (*She runs back to them and throws her arms around* FRANK'S *neck. They break apart and she puts one arm on* ANNE'S *shoulder, the other on* FRANK'S.) San Francisco is only fifty-five minutes away.

FRANK. We know. (*Smiles at her.*) Just around the corner. (MOLLIE *nods, then goes slowly to rejoin* ALEX. *They go off.* FRANK *and* ANNE *stand for a moment in silence.*) Annie, looking back, I can see now, it was just a question of growing up. That's all it was.

ANNE. (*Links her arm through his.*) You know there were times, Frank, when I never thought you would. (*As he turns and looks at her:*)

THE CURTAIN IS DOWN

PROPERTY PLOT

ACT ONE

SCENE 1—Graduation
On Stage Right Up and Down stage platform
Stage Left:
3 Folding chairs (Light oak)
Stage Right:
1 White and gold trimmed pedestal
1 White basket of mixed gladiolas

SCENE 2
No furniture here. Hand props listed on Hand prop list.

SCENE 2-A—Airport Gate
On Right side of fence
  1 White sign with Number and on it.
  1 Black ticket taker's stand.

SCENE 3—Living Room
Stage Right Platform working on and off stage
  1 Planter box with green ferns
  3 potted ferns
  1 Castered sofa
  1 Castered hassock
  3 throw pillows
  2 Light oak end tables
  2 Table lamps
  2 Black cane chairs with wicker seats
  1 Radio and Stereo combination
  1 Brass oval bar with marble top and shelf
Set dressing for this scene:
On bar:
  1 martini pitcher with stirrer
  6 martini glasses
  3 old fashioned glasses
  1 ice bucket with ice tongs
  1 bottle of gin unlabeled
  1 bottle of vermouth
  1 bottle of Bell scotch
On lower shelf:
  1 bottle of vodka
  1 bottle of liqueur

On top of Radio-Stereo:
  1 bowl (yellow) assorted flowers
  1 green bound book
Stage Right end table
  1 Webster's dictionary
  1 "Rise and Fall of the Third Reich"
  1 Ronson table lighter
  1 black ash tray
On stage Left End Table:
  1 beige Princess type telephone
  1 telephone note book with ball point pen
  1 package of Winston cigarettes

SCENE 4—Dormitory

  2 Twin-size type beds
  2 mattresses
  2 pillows
  2 straight backed chairs (Oak finish)
  1 Mahogany desk
  1 Poster (Bull Fight)
Set dressing for this scene:
On desk:
  1 portable typewriter
  1 glass jar with pencils
  1 black telephone (cradle type)
  1 desk lamp
  1 ash tray
  1 sketch book
  1 steno pad
  7 cloth bound books (college type)
  1 letter and envelope
Under desk:
  1 portable typewriter case
On stage Right bed:
  1 plaid (beige) bed spread
  1 small stuffed toy dog
On stage Left bed:
  1 plaid (beige) bed spread
  1 cigarette ash tray
  1 orange blouse
  1 orange skirt
On Center stage chair:
  1 white woolen sweater

Next to stage Right bed
 1 orange (grass weaved) waste paper basket

Scene 1-5—Living Room
Same as Scene 1-3

Scene 1-6—Dormitory

Furniture same as 1-4
Set dressing:
 White sweater is struck
 Letter and envelope
On Stage Right chair:
 1 green blouse

Scene 1-7—The Wall

No furniture here.
Hand props on Hand Prop list.

Scene 1-8—Living Room

Remains the same as 1-3 and 1-5.

Scene 1-9—Dormitory
Same as 1-6.

Scene 1-10—Living Room
Same as Scene 1-8

Yellow bowl of flowers is replaced by green bowl of assorted flowers.

Scene 1-11—Street Scene

Stage Left:
 1 Mail box.

Scene 1-12—Restaurant

 2 Gold pedestals
 2 Brass flower pots with palms
 1 2-foot diameter round table with gold base
 4 goldcane chairs with wicker seats
Set dressing for this scene:
On table:
 4 lobster plates with lobsters
 4 colored glasses (amber)
 4 paper napkins (white)
 4 lobster forks
 4 dinner forks
 4 dinner knives
 4 tea spoons

Scene 1-13—Living Room

Furniture the same.
Set dressing same, with artist's easel, palette, artist brush and one yard stick added.

Scene 1-14—Dormitory

Furniture same.

Set dressing:

Green blouse is struck.

Orange blouse and skirt are struck.

One striped (black and tan) sweater on Stage Left bed.

One imitation orange on same bed.

One box of blue writing paper and ball point pen also on same bed.

Scene 1-15—Bench

1 Bench (green) no back. Size: 4 feet long, 1 foot wide, 18" high.

Scene 1-16—Street

No furniture here.

Scene 1-17—Living Room

Furniture same as 1-13.

Set dressing:

Artist easel, palette, brush and yard stick are struck here.

Green bowl of flowers is replaced by white bowl of holly and pines.

Christmas wreath hung in center window.

Christmas packages (7 assorted sizes) on radio-stereo combination.

"Rise and Fall of the Third Reich" on Stage Left end table.

Scene 1-18—Dressing Table

1 dressing table with white skirt

1 dressing table bench

Scene 1-19—Living Room

Furniture same as 1-17

Set dressing same, with Christmas packages on radio-stereo struck.

ACT TWO

Scene 1—In One

No furniture used here.

Scene 2—Dormitory

Same as 1-4

Set dressing:

2 Guitars

Red bedspreads (folded) over foot of beds

Red pants over Stage Left bed

Strike orange waste paper basket

SCENE 3—Living Room
Same as Scene 1-3

Set dressing:
Christmas wreath, white bowl with holly and pines struck.
Webster's dictionary, flat package with 45 rpm record and
letter placed on Stage Left end of sofa.

SCENE 4—Sleeping Pill

3 15" diameter pedestal type tables
2 20" diameter pedestal type tables
2 gold cane chairs (padded seats)
1 gold cane chair (wicker seat)
4 cane chairs
2 wire chairs
2 wire 36" high backed stools
1 black cane chair (wicker seat)

Set dressing:
5 assorted bottles with candles
3 white coffee cups
3 white napkins
1 Home made menu

SCENE 5—In One

No furniture used here.

SCENE 6—Classroom

1 Oak desk
5 Light oak tabloid arm chair
1 Oak armchair
1 Oak blackboard

Set dressing:
On the desk:
3 hard bound books on right side of desk
1 book of poems
1 man's handkerchief
On blackboard:
1 chalk eraser and chalk (white)

SCENE 7—In One

No furniture used here.

SCENE 8—Dormitory

Furniture same as 2-2.

Set dressing:
Center stage chair 1 blue dress draped over it.
On desk:
Belt from dress
1 evening bag (Lady's)

Lady's shoes on floor next to Center Stage chair
Portable typewriter, not used in the second act.

Scene 9—Wall

No furniture used here.

Scene 10—Barbecue

1 wrought iron table
1 wrought iron hassock
2 wire high backed chairs
1 wire high bracket armchair
1 barbecue (with hood)

Set dressing:
   All chairs have blue and white checked seat pads
   Hassock has blue and white checked pad
   Barbecue tools hung from barbecue.

Scene 11—Airport Gate

Same as Scene 1-2A
Black ticket taker's stand.

HAND PROPS

ACT ONE

Graduation—Stage Right:
No hand props.
Stage Left:
1 Man's wrist watch (Frank)
Airport—Stage Right:
1 Lady's wrist watch
1 Hard bound book
1 American Airlines ticket
1 Blue bag (shapeless)
1 Beige dressing case
2 Women's magazines
1 Box of Nabisco cookies
1 Woman's tan trenchcoat
Stage Left:
1 Book of poetry "Sonnets From The Portuguese"
Airport Gate—Stage Right:
1 Clipboard with passenger list
1 Ball point pen
1 Man's wrist watch
1 Coca-Cola paper cup with Coke in it
1 Small bottle of pills
Stage Left:
No hand props
Living Room—Stage Right:
1 Small bowl of fruit (apples)
1 Black cigarette ash tray
Dormitory:
Hand props used in this scene are part of set dressing and are
    itemized under Set Dressing.
Living Room—Stage Right:
Several letters
1 Special letter from Mollie
Stage Left:
No hand props
Dormitory—Stage Right:
No hand props
Stage Left:
Cigarettes
Cigarette holder

Cigarette lighter

All other hand props used in this scene are listed under Set Dressing as they are part of the set.

Wall—Stage Right:

No hand props

Stage Left:

1 Package of cigarettes

1 Cigarette lighter

Living Room—Stage Right:

1 Special letter (continuation of 1st placed on set for Frank)

Stage Left:

No hand props

Dormitory—Stage Right:

Stage Left:

1 Bottle of nail polish

All other props are part of Set Dressing and are noted under Set Dressing.

Living Room—Stage Right—Stage Left:

Hand props used are part of Set Dressing and are noted under Set Dressing.

Street Scene—Stage Right:

1 Letter for Frank Michaelson

Stage Left:

1 Portable radio

Restaurant—Stage Right—Stage Left:

All props used in this scene are part of the Set Dressing and are listed under Set Dressing.

Living Room—Stage Right—Stage Left:

All props used in this scene are part of the Set Dressing and are listed under Set Dressing.

Dormitory—Stage Right—Stage Left:

All props used in this scene are part of set dressing and are so listed.

Bench Scene—Stage Right:

No hand props

Stage Left:

1 Woman's purse

1 Compact

1 Lipstick

1 Woman's comb

Street Scene—Stage Right—Stage Left:

No hand props used in this scene.

Living Room—Stage Right:
1 Beige dressing case
1 Blue bag (Shapeless)
1 Cigarette holder (woman's)
1 Cigarette (Winston)
Matches
1 Large basket of assorted flowers
All other props used in this scene are part of Set Dressing and
   are so noted.

Stage Left:
No hand props.

Dressing Table—Stage Right:
1 Gold sweater (girl's)
1 star made of aluminum foil

Stage Left:
1 Turkish (beige) sewed as head turban   Towel

Living Room—Stage Right—Stage Left:
All hand props used in this scene are part of set dressing and
   are so noted.

ACT TWO

Played in One—Stage Right—Stage Left:
No hand props used in this scene.

Dormitory—Stage Right—Stage Left:
All hand props used in this scene are placed on the set and are
   listed under Set Dressing.

Living Room—Stage Right—Stage Left:
All hand props used in this scene are placed on the set and are
   listed under Set Dressing.

Sleeping Pill—Stage Right:
1 Ball point pen
1 Piece of white paper used as note paper

Stage Left:
1 Large white apron
1 9" pizza pie
1 9" white plate
2 white coffee cups
2 Guitars
1 Knife
1 Dinner fork
1 Tea spoon

In One—Stage Right:
No hand props

Stage Left:
1 Sketch book
1 Hard bound book
1 Small paper bound book
Classroom—Stage Right—Stage Left:
Same books as used in 2-5
1 Man's handkerchief
1 Man's eye glasses
All other hand props used are part of the set dressing and are so noted.
In One—Stage Right:
1 Sketch book
1 Hard bound book
1 Small paper bound book
Stage Left:
No hand props
Dormitory—Stage Right
Stage Left:
1 Bottle of mouth wash
1 Yellow plastic cup
1 Lady's cigarette holder
Cigarettes
Cigarette lighter
All other props used are part of the Set Dressing and are so noted.
Wall—Stage Right:
1 Hard bound book of poetry
Stage Left:
1 Large sketch book
1 Hard bound book
1 Paper bound book (small)
1 Sheaf of green leaves
Barbecue—Stage Right:
1 Steno type machine
1 Los Angeles newspaper
2 Highball glasses with ice cubes and liquid
Stage Left:
1 Platter of steaks
Airport Gate—Stage Right:
1 Man's trenchcoat
1 Clipboard with passenger list
1 Ball point pen
1 Man's wrist watch

Stage Left:
1 Lady's trenchcoat
2 Lady's magazines
1 Blue dressing case
1 Brown bag (shapeless)
2 American Airlines tickets
1 American Airlines blue bag
1 Box of Nabisco cookies
1 Man's trenchcoat

COSTUME PLOT

FRANK MICHAELSON:
Undre dress
Blue Ban-lon Shirt

Dark gray suit
Blue Oxford shirt
Striped tie
Black loafers

Sport Jacket

Yellow sweater
Tan slacks
Gray and white striped sweater

White shirt
Tan car coat

Black dress suit
Turba

Brown slacks
White shirt
Tan cardigan

Gray light-weight suit
White shirt, tie
Gray overcoat and hat

Yellow sport shirt checked
Light sport slacks
Brown shoes
Tan sport jacket

MOLLIE MICHAELSON:
White graduation gown and cap

Yellow plaid suit
Yellow hat
Tan pocketbook

Tan shoes
Yellow coat

Blue polka dot pajamas
Blue furred bedroom slippers

Mustard and plaid wool dress
Tan low-heeled shoes

Repeat pajamas
Gold corduroy robe
Same slippers

Light green silk dress
Tan velvet jacket
Satin evening bag
Black high heel shoes

Black dress
Black coat
Leopard trimmed
Muff
Black high heeled shoes
Pearl necklace
Long pearl earrings

Red velvet dress, pink lace top
Red velvet jacket
Black shoes

Light grey slacks
Striped sweater, light blue trim
Flat boots

Beatnik dress, black and henna
Black tights
Black flats
Long beads

Checked Wool dress
Rust colored coat
Low-heeled tan shoes

Pre-set blue silk dress
Black high heel shoes
Blue evening bag

Lavender Wool skirt
Striped mohair sweater
Tan sport shoes

Pink cotton wool dress
Matching jacket, white trim
Tan high heel shoes
Small tan hand bag

LIZ MICHAELSON:
Green print white background dress, blue jacket
White silk low-heeled shoes
Short white gloves
Hair ribbons

Burgundy slacks
Gold cotton blouse
White sneakers

Tan plaid short skirt
Rust colored sweater
Sneakers

Two-piece blue wool dress
White blouse
Green car coat
Sneakers

Blue denim jeans
Mustard colored sweat shirt
Sneakers

Blue plaid wool suit with green top
Green felt hat
Black kid shoes

ANNE MICHAELSON:
Green linen dress
White jacket, green trim

Tan shoes
Tan hand bag
Pearls

Pink linen skirt over blouse
Jacket

Pink sweater

Blue linen two-piece dress
Black shoes

Blue linen skirt
Blue Paisley blouse
Small print apron

Orange wool dress
Yellow wool coat
Tan hand bag
Tan shoes

Beige satin and lace dress
Long pearl earrings
Beige satin shoes

Green linen dress
Blue sweater

Shocking pink slacks
Flowered silk blouse
Black flat shoes

Light tan linen dress
Checked linen jacket, white trim
Tan bag and shoes

ALEX LOOMIS
Black suit
White shirt
Tie
Black shoes

Sport jacket

Blue shirt
Gray slacks

Oxford gray suit
White shirt
Tie

Tan slacks
French blue shirt
Dark sweater
Loafers

ADELE MCDOUGALL:
Tan wool skirt
Bright orange cotton blouse
High wool socks
Loafers

Pajamas, blue and white print
Tan furred bedroom slippers

Blue velvet dress and jacket
Black shoes, high heels
Two strand pearls

Dark burgundy Paisley blouse
Two-piece pale blue jersey dress
Loafers

SARAH WALKER:
Dark red wool turtleneck blouse
Shocking pink wool sleeveless dress
Dark red shoes
Gold necklace

Blue wool robe

Repeat pink dress
Maroon cape
Handbag

Striped multi-colored wool dress
Same shoes

Dark red pleated silk dress

Gold wool dress
Gold necklace

LINDA LEHMAN:
Toupe slacks
Red Paisley blouse
Green bulky sweater

Beatnik dress
Black tights
Black flat shoes
Three long strings of beads

PRINCIPAL:
Gray business suit
White shirt
Striped tie
Black shoes and socks

AIR LINE CLERK:
Blue uniform and cap
White shirt, black tie
Black shoes

EMMETT:
Pale blue jeans
White tee shirt
Sneakers
White wool socks

Tweed suit
Striped shirt
Dark tie

Gray-blue messenger suit and cap
Black shoes and socks

Dark grey business suit
White shirt, tie
Black shoes

DONN BOWDRY
  Blue jacket
  Tan shirt, tie
  Gold wool vest
  Dark slacks
  Brown loafers

  Dark suit
  White shirt
  Black shoes and socks

1ST FRESHMAN
  Dark plaid shirt
  Chinoes, light green
  Warm brown sweater
  Blue lumber jacket
  Sport shoes
  Black socks

2ND FRESHMAN:
  Dark gray slacks
  White shirt, dark tie
  Brown leather shoes
  Black socks
  Green and gray stripe sweater

RICHARD GLUCK:
  Tweed sport jacket
  Striped shirt
  Olive green slacks cords
  Royal blue and black sweater

ALFRED GREIFFINGER:
  Yellow shirt
  Light tan chinoes
  Green bulky sweater
  High top loafers
  White socks

CLANCY:
  Black linen slacks
  Black turtle neck sweater
  Gold shirt

Black striped cardigan
Black shoes and socks

MR. HIBBETTS :
Brown tweed suit
Blue Oxford shirt
Bow tie
Black shoes and socks

MR. WHITMYER :
Gray striped business suit
White shirt, tie
Black shoes

OTHER TITLES AVAILABLE FROM SAMUEL FRENCH

SKIN DEEP
Jon Lonoff

Comedy / 2m, 2f / Interior Unit Set
In *Skin Deep*, a large, lovable, lonely-heart, named Maureen Mulligan, gives romance one last shot on a blind-date with sweet awkward Joseph Spinelli; she's learned to pepper her speech with jokes to hide insecurities about her weight and appearance, while he's almost dangerously forthright, saying everything that comes to his mind. They both know they're perfect for each other, and in time they come to admit it.

They were set up on the date by Maureen's sister Sheila and her husband Squire, who are having problems of their own: Sheila undergoes a non-stop series of cosmetic surgeries to hang onto the attractive and much-desired Squire, who may or may not have long ago held designs on Maureen, who introduced him to Sheila. With Maureen particularly vulnerable to both hurting and being hurt, the time is ripe for all these unspoken issues to bubble to the surface.

"Warm-hearted comedy ... the laughter was literally show-stopping. A winning play, with enough good-humored laughs and sentiment to keep you smiling from beginning to end."
– *TalkinBroadway.com*

"It's a little Paddy Chayefsky, a lot Neil Simon and a quick-witted, intelligent voyage into the not-so-tranquil seas of middle-aged love and dating. The dialogue is crackling and hilarious; the plot simple but well-turned; the characters endearing and quirky; and lurking beneath the merriment is so much heartache that you'll stand up and cheer when the unlikely couple makes it to the inevitable final clinch."
– *NYTheatreWorld.Com*

OTHER TITLES AVAILABLE FROM SAMUEL FRENCH

COCKEYED
William Missouri Downs

Comedy / 3m, 1f / Unit Set

Phil, an average nice guy, is madly in love with the beautiful Sophia. The only problem is that she's unaware of his existence. He tries to introduce himself but she looks right through him. When Phil discovers Sophia has a glass eye, he thinks that might be the problem, but soon realizes that she really can't see him. Perhaps he is caught in a philosophical hyperspace or dualistic reality or perhaps beautiful women are just unaware of nice guys. Armed only with a B.A. in philosophy, Phil sets out to prove his existence and win Sophia's heart. This fast moving farce is the winner of the HotCity Theatre's GreenHouse New Play Festival. The St. Louis Post-Dispatch called Cockeyed a clever romantic comedy, Talkin' Broadway called it "hilarious," while Playback Magazine said that it was "fresh and invigorating."

Winner!
of the HotCity Theatre GreenHouse New Play Festival

"Rocking with laughter...hilarious...polished and engaging work draws heavily on the age-old conventions of farce: improbable situations, exaggerated characters, amazing coincidences, absurd misunderstandings, people hiding in closets and barely missing each other as they run in and out of doors...full of comic momentum as Cockeyed hurtles toward its conclusion."
–Talkin' Broadway

NO SEX PLEASE, WE'RE BRITISH
Anthony Marriott and Alistair Foot

Farce / 7 m, 3 f / Interior

A young bride who lives above a bank with her husband who is the assistant manager, innocently sends a mail order off for some Scandinavian glassware. What comes is Scandinavian pornography. The plot revolves around what is to be done with the veritable floods of pornography, photographs, books, films and eventually girls that threaten to engulf this happy couple. The matter is considerably complicated by the man's mother, his boss, a visiting bank inspector, a police superintendent and a muddled friend who does everything wrong in his reluctant efforts to set everything right, all of which works up to a hilarious ending of closed or slamming doors. This farce ran in London over eight years and also delighted Broadway audiences.

"Titillating and topical."
– NBC TV

"A really funny Broadway show."
– ABC TV

OTHER TITLES AVAILABLE FROM SAMUEL FRENCH

BLUE YONDER
Kate Aspengren

Dramatic Comedy / Monolgues and scenes
12f (can be performed with as few as 4 with doubling) / Unit Set

A familiar adage states, "Men may work from sun to sun, but women's work is never done." In Blue Yonder, the audience meets twelve mesmerizing and eccentric women including a flight instructor, a firefighter, a stuntwoman, a woman who donates body parts, an employment counselor, a professional softball player, a surgical nurse professional baseball player, and a daredevil who plays with dynamite among others. Through the monologues, each woman examines her life's work and explores the career that she has found. Or that has found her.